FIRE OF AURORA: IDOLEX

VANESSA PARK

ISBN: 9798519645829

DEDICATION

For Katherine, who reminds me what it is to yearn.

CONTENTS

ACKNOWLEDGMENTS

This series owes an endless debt to Mister S, to The Man With The Inkless Pen, and to the infinite world machine of science-fiction imagination which has sprung from the collective consciousness of genre writers and dreamers in the last 150 years.

1 - FUEL

Ray Carson wore a nametag that said 'LOU.' It was the name he'd been given six years ago, when he'd cowered in the back of a chow mein spot to meet with the only identity broker he could find. The guy had done a good enough job. "'Lucky Lou Hastings,'" the broker had said, handing him a ticket on a third-class cruiser to the outworlds. Next came the ID card, birth certificate, and tax records of a 'Louis Hastings' who had died alone some two months prior.

All it had cost him was everything he owned, and everyone in the world he'd ever known. Ray took the four-day cruiser trip to Clanawley, weeping and snoring in intermittent bursts the whole time. By the time he arrived at the overcast hunk of space rock, population thirty-thousand and change, he had grown numb to the bleakness of his situation. Anything that befell him here, he thought, was still better than a life behind bars in some deep-space prison.

The broker had bought him a commercial fueling station on the corner of a dirt road and a gravel one. It was a big, open-lot business, the kind frequented by deep-space haulers and day-trippers who forgot to fuel up before the asteroid gap. Considering the charges he'd barely escaped,

Ray figured that buying him a fuel station must have been some kind of twisted joke on the part of the broker. He tried not to think about it too much.

The morning, like every other morning on Clanawley, was grey. Ray puffed a damp cigarette, shoving a key into the dew-covered lock of the fuel station office. Everything that came here turned damp and soft eventually. Even his tan suit and trousers, once pressed and starched in the crispest coreworld fashion, were descending with him into a state of lumpy decay.

An unfamiliar shuttle had landed on the farthest pad. It was strange to see a short-range craft at Value Fueling, since inevitably their host cruisers were the ones to land for mid-voyage resupply. It was also strange to see a shuttle parked on the farthest of twenty fueling pads. After all, the pilot would have to walk a good two minutes, past plenty of other open spots, to purchase his temporary fuel pass at the office.

A familiar couple distracted him from the sight of the navy-blue shuttle. "Two packs," said Rick Healey, smiling through chipped and yellowed teeth.

Ray grabbed Rick two packs of the usual cigs. On the other side of the glass, a grimy tube-topped girl hung on Rick Healey's arm, nibbling at the smoke-stained fabric of the man's worn-out hoodie. She looked like she could have been his daughter's age. With a needy tug, she glanced at Ray, then whispered something to Rick.

"Oh yeah," said Rick, "some condoms. The blue ones."

Ray slid a pack of condoms onto the security tray. "You've still got credit," he said, tapping through Rick Healey's account history. "Enjoy."

The girl hung off Rick's arm in sort of giddy stupor, smiling at Ray through the graffiti-scratched glass. Her overused tank top was loose, and it fell to reveal a pale pink nipple on her freckled breast. "I'll see you 'round, gas man," she laughed, and made a show of readjusting her top before Rick shoved her over to the sidewalk.

Ray Carson would never see her again. His soft blue eyes, turned grey by the deadened sky, squinted as he made out the form of a young man walking up to the window. The young man couldn't have been older than nineteen, clean-cut and strong with a lean athlete's build. He had short, tawny hair, and a well-cut face that shone with a mix of cheeriness and forthright conviction.

The young man was Miles Meyrich. He wore a grey, armored exo-suit, its servos whirring quietly with each step in Clanawley's mid-range gravity. On his hip was a custom-tuned Featherhand electromagnetic sidearm.

"You don't need that suit here, or that iron," said Ray. He never would have said 'iron' in his coreworld days, but the slow drawl of the locals and haulers had started to take hold of him.

"I do when I'm on duty," said Miles. "Gimme two thousand credits on pad twenty."

He flashed an emerald-level digi-wallet, which chimed green as it accepted the charge. *This kid's no small timer,* Ray thought. Then he caught something cagey in the young man's eye. "You're not just here for fuel, are you?" he asked.

Miles sighed a rehearsed sigh, like he'd been trying to figure out how to break some bad news the whole way over here. "No, sir, I'm not," said Miles. "I'm with Aurora Protective Services," you ever heard of us?

He flashed a fake business card, which Ray gazed at through the murky bulletproof glass. "Can't say I have," said the station owner.

"Yeah," said Miles, glancing up at the overcast sky. "Well, it's a big galaxy. I'm Miles Meyrich. What's your name, man?"

Ray prickled at this. The question always dug at his flabby, fugitive guts. "Lou," he said, tapping his nametag with indignation. "Isn't it obvious?"

"Sure," said Miles. "Lou Hastings, right? I just gotta be sure. See, we picked up a thief a few million clicks from here, stranded just past the inner edge of the belt. He'd been joyriding one of our client's favorite race shuttles. Unfortunately, we also found record of three million credits in currency hacks from various vendors in this region, including about eight-hundred thousand from your fuel station's account. The money was all crypto-signed, and he blew most of it before we found him, so there's not a whole lot we can do about recovery."

Ray's skin turned cold at the news. He'd barely been able to afford this place after the broker's fees. There was no way he could survive starting again. "Ridiculous," he said, letting optimistic skepticism take control. "You must have the wrong place. I just checked our balances this morning, everything's there."

"Sometimes the blockchain takes a few days to post large transfers out here," said Miles. "I'd love to say we've got the wrong place, but..." He held up a handset with the employer identification code of Value Fueling displayed. "This is your business, right?"

Ray's hands went clammy, and his neck cold. It was a feeling he hadn't suffered since his days on Coronaire, when he'd been terrified of a republic anti-crime team breaking through his window each night as he went to sleep. "How can this happen?" he stuttered, indignant and terrified. "Nobody's been in here. I've checked the cameras—"

Miles made a show of checking the time on his suit's wrist computer. "There are some things we can try," he said. "I've got a little time before I gotta get back. Listen, first, can I use your bathroom?"

"No restroom for customers," Ray said reflexively. Then he changed his tone. "Of course, under these circumstances, it's fine, of course. Please, come in."

He put his hand on the biometric scanner that unlocked the outer office door. Then he turned the key to release the deadbolt. "Mind that suit on the carpet," he said, as the young man with the pistol on his hip stepped inside.

The next moment, Miles' sidearm barrel was pressed into Ray's temple. Ray didn't jump, or scream, or do anything except stare at the tawny-haired kid in muddled confusion. It all just happened too fast. "Ray Carson?" said Miles, grabbing the man's thumb and scanning its print with his handset. "You're wanted by the Systems Republic for fraud, embezzlement, illegal storage of torchdrive fuel, and eighty-nine counts of negligent homicide."

"I don't know a Ray Carson," said Ray, so panicked he could barely breathe. "What is this, a stick up? Where's my money?"

"It's all there," said Miles, pointing to his digital till. "You better hope you can use it on a good lawyer, Ray. You shoulda done that from the start instead of skipping town."

"And the stolen racer?"

Miles scoffed. He opened the door to the lot again, walking Ray out into the cloudy morning with a pistol to his back. "There's no racer," he said. "Dude, c'mon. Think a little. I was lying so you would open the security door."

Ray gritted his teeth as he felt the gun at his back. With each step toward the young man's navy-blue shuttle, he considered turning to fight. Even a bullet to the gut would be better than the sentence that awaited him back home. Then he heard the young man wobble and heave.

"Hang on," said Miles, sounding newly queasy. "Oh, I, uh, wow. I think I'm gonna be sick. Hang on."

Miles put a hand up, urging his prisoner to stay put. He leaned over and heaved on the fueling pad asphalt. Then, with a splotchy paleness to his face, he collapsed to the ground in a daze.

Ray Carson blinked, staring down at the nausea-stricken bounty hunter. *Is this some kind of test?* Then he glanced at his own parked ship a few dozen yards away.

It didn't take long before the suited man was sprinting off toward his getaway ride. "Ray!" he heard Miles shout between dry heaves. "Ray, c'mon. Don't make this bad."

Ray had no mind to grant him any sort of gentlemanly time-out. He dug through his pockets, finding his keys, and clicked a button to start the motor of the two-engine passenger ship just as he reached it. "Oh, fuck," was his constant gasp as he clambered into the pilot's seat. "Oh, fuck. Oh, fuck. Oh, fuck."

Then he saw the red-and-black armored woman on the outside of the cockpit glass. She was standing by the port engine, on the tarmac of the fueling pad. At first, she seemed confused by the vehicle's sudden start. Then she noticed Ray at the controls. "Hey!" she shouted, barely audible through the engine roar and the space-rated glass. "Hey, stop!"

Ray didn't want to crush her. He also didn't want to wait one more second for her to get out of the way. Gritting his teeth, he pushed the throttle forward, expecting to hear a terrible scrape as the spacesuited woman was ground up under the wing.

That crunch never came. There was a slight jolt of acceleration, then a teeth-shaking clang, and all at once the ship was stuck hovering ten feet up.

The woman had attached an anchor chain from the ground to the bottom of the craft. It groaned, metal straining as Ray pushed the throttle harder and harder. Try as he might, he couldn't get it to snap. Then he heard a new set of thuds on the side of the cockpit.

The woman in the red and black spacesuit was climbing the outside of the glass. "Ray!" she shouted, amplified by the speakers of her suit as she hung from the cockpit's metal frame. "Put the ship down!"

Ray pushed the throttle to max. He could hear the anchor grinding as it tried to tear away from the asphalt and bedrock. *Any second now, I'll be free.*

Then broken glass rained down on him. Through screaming engine noise, the woman in the suit punched through the cockpit windscreen. Like a caged tiger, she pried at the frame, twisting it open with her servo-assisted strength. "Holy fuck!" Ray shouted, partially deafened by the thruster outside.

The woman yanked Ray Carson out of his pilot's chair. She jumped backward with him in her arms, and after a ten foot drop the two landed with a suit-softened thud on spongey asphalt. "KALI!" she shouted, presumably to someone on her comms. "Get that fucking ship shut down! Put an override through."

Ray couldn't hear the response, but a moment later his twin-engine ship went dead. It hung in mid-air, connected to the ground by its anchor chain like a steel balloon. Then with a crash it fell back down to the pavement.

The woman knelt on Ray Carson's back, grabbing his wrists and applying magnetic cuffs. He tasted the tarry asphalt as his stunned face pressed against it. He heard her helmet come off, and a sigh of exertion as the young man with the pistol approached.

"Captain," said the young man, apology and embarrassment in his tone.

"Miles," said the woman in the suit. "What happened?"

"I dunno, ma'am," said Miles. "Everything just went hazy. But I'm fine now."

"No you're not," said the captain. "Go sit down. I'll wrap this jailbird up. Soon as we get back to *Aurora*, I want you to report to Mia Rain for a full evaluation."

* * *

Evelyn Miyachi watched welding sparks fly on the crossbeams of the shuttle bay bulkhead. "Higher," she said, pointing to a place where *Aurora's* steel-composite frame needed reinforcement. Ten yards ahead and ten feet up, April Zamora operated the powerful torch in a welding mask and an orange blast-proof jumpsuit.

Evelyn could have finished the job much faster than April. Her seven-foot, cybernetically reinforced body could scale the gantry up to the welding site with ease. Her nanotube-striated muscles could have held the torch in one hand, and her clear-plated eyes could have watched the burn without any fear of damage. Still, April had to learn. The whole point of a junior chief engineer was to have a redundant expert on deck, in case the worst ever befell Evelyn.

The smooth, robotic voice of the ship's navigational intelligence came through *Aurora's* shuttle bay intercom. "Shuttle *Sanpi* approaching rear lock," said KALI. "Clear bay for docking."

April looked down at Evelyn. Even through the junior engineer's formless jumpsuit and mask, Evelyn could see that she was exhausted. "I can finish it," said Evelyn. "Dismissed, Zamora."

April nodded, lowering the torch to the floor with a motorized winch. Then she stowed it in a magnetized cage along with the helmet and gloves. Reddened marks shone on her tan, grease-smeared face where the mask had pressed it. In the shuttle bay light, her lip and nose rings shimmered cool blue. Her hazel eyes scanned Evelyn with a reader's intuition as she pushed her purple hair back.

April's status as a reader made things easier for Evelyn. The cyborg had trouble with niceties, and in her brusqueness she often gave the false impression of anger. April Zamora, who could see at least slightly into the emotions of others, never had to deal with the friction of such misunderstanding.

"I'll clear out," said April, speaking in the accent of an urban outworlder. You could not have found a voice more different from Evelyn's cool contemplation.

"I'll stay," said Evelyn, and lay a hand on a support column for balance.

Overhead, a red light flashed, indicating that *Sanpi* was waiting to dock. "Scram," said Captain Amestoy's voice, piped to the hangar intercom from the shuttle cockpit. "I've got a sick boy in need of a doctor's loving touch."

April left the shuttle bay, and the breathable air began to drain from the room. Evelyn loved the feeling of being in vacuum. Across her body, the nanomachines inside her began to activate, switching her cellular processes from oxygen-based respiration to internal power. It started from her chest, spreading out in a broadening wave. Her tongue, nipples, and vulva were the most sensitive to the change, and she shivered as she felt the machines inside them whir.

In silence, the bay door opened. Evelyn could see the blackness of space below, and the cloudy skies of the microplanet Clanawley swirling under terraformer fields. The only sense of sound was the rumble which ran through the ship's steel pillar into her sensitive fingers.

Sanpi rose up into the ship, and the bay doors closed. Then the six-seater shuttle set down and the air returned. Evelyn, in her orange engineer's fatigues, was usually the first to greet the away teams just by virtue of being in the hangar. This time, Captain Amestoy emerged in her trademark red-and-black armor, pushing a tan-suited middle-aged man forward.

"Have Lex put this one in the brig," said Amestoy, fluffing up her short-bobbed black hair after removing her helmet. The captain was tall, with desert-tan skin and athletic build complemented by her full bust. Even in the field, she wore lipstick and liner, and her eyes always moved with a sharp and piercing boldness.

On cue, *Aurora* enforcer Lex Rockbridge entered, flashing gold teeth as he took the prisoner's arm in a beefy hand. "Have a nice getaway?" he asked the dejected man as he led him away.

Then Miles Meyrich exited the shuttle, a smile on his pale and perpetually cleanshaven face. He didn't look too sick to Evelyn. Then again, she didn't have much familiarity with various ailments of unaltered humans.

"Go to the med bay," said Amestoy, with a light and almost mothering tone. "Now."

"Yes, ma'am," said Miles, and nodded to Evelyn before leaving. It was clear that he still had no idea what to make of the quiet, contemplative cyborg engineer.

Amestoy lingered a moment in front of Evelyn. "You're an unusual soul, Miss Miyachi," said the captain. "I'd love to find you another unusual someone."

Evelyn stared at the captain, processing a response. In her head, blurry images of imaginary partners flickered and smiled, somewhere in between a simulation and a daydream. She'd considered such things, but never seriously. She couldn't imagine a human being looking at her in passion.

"Perhaps someday," she said at last to her captain. "I have more than enough to keep me busy in the meantime."

Amestoy's handset chirped, and she quickly unlocked it.

"Well, let's put a pin in it," said the captain, quickly stripping out of her armor and down to her black neoprene undersuit. "Speaking of someones, I'm late."

2 - PASTIME

Corrine Amestoy climbed the stairs to her captain's quarters on the top level of her privateer cruiser *Aurora*. The thirty-bunk ship's common floors were constantly alive with murmur and idle conversation. Her deck, on the other hand, was always serenely quiet—except for the moans of her guests.

Grace Burdette was already waiting for her, lying atop the comforter in a white dress with matching go-go boots. Grace's skin was soft and polished, and her platinum bob shone with the glow of expensive conditioner as sat up reading through some legal brief.

She set the brief aside as Amestoy entered. "I see you've been dying here waiting for me," said the captain, cracking sarcasm at the woman who was both her lawyer and sexual property.

"I *have* been dying for you," said Grace, pressing her hand against her crotch through her dress. "Want to feel?"

"Let me shower and I'll be there," said Amestoy, starting to unzip the front of her damp undersuit.

"I like you like that," said Grace, touching a boot-tip to Amestoy's thigh where it leaned against the foot of the master bed. The sheets, like everything else in this former yacht's best suite, were built to luxurious spec.

"That rock smells like a cold sauna," said Amestoy, climbing up to kneel in the center of the bed. "But alright, you can have me."

She put an undersuit-gloved hand on the back of Grace's head, guiding the woman to smell the salt and sweat at her navel. She took care not to muss Grace's hair as she handled her. Each time, Grace Burdette arrived like a gift, beautifully done-up as a box from a diamond store might be. Amestoy didn't want to rip her apart too fast.

With a long, yearning lick, Grace put her tongue on the undersuit, feeling Amestoy's abs flex beneath the spongey material. Then the captain flicked on a holo-display on the suite's far wall.

The whole wall illuminated as one giant interface. Amestoy's desktop appeared, with a picture of vintage race-shuttle pilot Antonia Ghidella roaring in topless, champagne-soaked victory as the background. Atop the black-and-white image of the racer, a few dozen stray notes and files cluttered the view.

Amestoy dismissed them all with a wrist-flick. "I found someone," she told Grace, rubbing her finger where the jewels of the lawyer's golden ear-cuff met her earlobe. "We've been messaging. You'll like her."

"Yes, ma'am," said Grace, whose breathing was shaky with anticipation.

Captain Amestoy let the zipper of her undersuit down a little more. "KALI," she said, and the shipboard intelligence chimed with understanding. "Get Lydia McNeil from my contacts on the wall here."

"Yes, captain," said KALI, and a call screen appeared on the far wall with a soft ring. At all four corners, the room's holo-scanners whirred as they brought the women on the bed into focus.

A brown-haired woman in her forties appeared on screen. She wore a professional blouse, and the makeup of someone who'd just returned from a day at a coreworld office. Behind her, in clear view on the holo-field display, was a home office cluttered with boxes, clothes, and mail.

Amestoy could hear shuttles on the other side, through the woman's second-floor window. With a plain and confident smile, the captain raised a hand to the mid-level executive on the screen. "Hi Lydia," she said. "It's good to meet you. I'm Corrine, and this is Grace."

"Hi," said Lydia McNeil, already blushing with embarrassment. Amestoy watched her glance to the closed office door as two small steps of footsteps ran past.

"Your kids?" Amestoy asked, putting her hand on the small of Grace's back and stroking it.

"Yeah," said Lydia. "Six and eight. Do you have any kids? Well, no, I imagine you don't, I mean, I would think."

"No kids," said Amestoy.

Lydia listened again to the footsteps, then turned on a fan for some white noise. "They're with their sitter," she said. "My husband's not home. He doesn't exactly know, I mean, that we've been talking. He doesn't know about any of this."

"Does that turn you on?" asked Amestoy.

The woman blushed, exhaling as she turned her face away. Then she nodded. "Yeah," she said, like no one had asked her that in a long time. "Yeah it does."

"I want you to open your shirt up," said Amestoy. All

the while, Grace leaned against her, running manicured fingers in circles on her inner thigh. "Let me see the body you've been hiding."

The woman adjusted in her chair. Then, with care, she undid the top four buttons of her shirt, revealing a beige underwire bra beneath. Her sternum was flecked faint sunspots, flushed above a soft and pale bosom which moved as she breathed.

"You like men, Lydia?" Amestoy asked.

Each thing the captain said seemed to surprise the woman, and draw her attention ever nearer. "Yes," said Lydia. "Yes, I do."

"But you like women, too," said Amestoy.

"Yes," said Lydia. "I think so. I think I have, always."

Amestoy gestured to adjust the breadth of her holo-scanners, focusing in on Grace Burdette, so the lawyer would appear like an immaculate living portrait on Lydia's home office holo-display. "What do you think of Grace?" Amestoy asked, touching the woman's sharp jaw with her gloved hand to show her off.

"She's beautiful," said Lydia McNeil, with the hush of admitting a high school crush.

"Where do you work, Lydia?" Amestoy asked.

"I work in finance, on Pleiana," said Lydia. "I do estimations for new sub-orbital construction."

Now Amestoy turned to the woman on the bed beside her. "Grace," she said, "if you saw Mrs. McNeil at an office party on Pleiana, what would you want to do?"

Grace gazed at the kind, yearning face of the woman on the holo-screen. There was a deep and intelligent passion long dormant beneath the slim creases of her suburban countenance. "I would want to kiss her," said Grace.

Lydia gave a light, touched smile as the imagined scenario filled her. "And would you?" Amestoy asked, putting a fingertip to Grace's shining lips.

"No," said Grace. "I'd be too shy."

"And what would you say to her at that stupid party, if you knew?" Amestoy asked Lydia. "If you were a reader and you knew what she wanted, what would you say?"

Lydia swallowed. "Hello," she said, bashful and intimate in the confines of the fantasy.

"Hello," said Grace, staring into her eyes across the distance.

"Take her somewhere," said Amestoy, guiding.

Lydia laughed softly as she imagined it. "There's a statue by Satoshi Fujima on the next floor up," she said to Grace. "I have a passcard. Would you like to see it?"

"I would," whispered Grace.

"Who's up there?" asked Amestoy, pulling Grace closer with a smile.

"No one," said Lydia. "Just us. The lights are off. But the whole floor is lit by the billboards on the Bayren Building, through the windows."

"What color?" asked Grace, turning her eyes from the screen to her captain.

"Red," said Lydia.

With a touch to a dial, Captain Amestoy shifted the cabin lights to a rich red. In that glow, she joined Grace within the holo-frame, holding her neck as she kissed the blonde-bobbed woman.

They pressed their bodies close, warm with each other's spit as they pushed their lips and tongues together. "I want you," Grace murmured, kissing at Amestoy's neck and jaw.

"All of this is for you."

Amestoy unzipped her undersuit to below her navel, pulling her arms from the sleeves and letting it fall around her waist. The moisture on her full breasts shone in the red light as she cradled Grace, who sucked at her hard, dark nipple with devotion. "Take your shirt off, Lydia," said Amestoy, repositioning Grace for a tighter hold. "Your bra, too. That door's locked, right?"

"Yeah," said Lydia, breathless as she undid her front-clasp bra and tossed her shirt back against the office chair. Her own nipples were hard and pink, bathed in the glow of afternoon coreworld sun from the nearby window.

Amestoy felt a hot pulse in her crotch as she watched the financial executive strip down.

Lydia swallowed, working up the nerve to let her secret desires come alive. "Do you think you could—"

"Touch yourself," Amestoy interrupted, commanding. As she said it, she pushed Grace's soft hand toward her own trimmed vulva. Sliding back in her chair, Lydia McNeil unbuttoned her pants and started rubbing her clit the way she'd learned so many years ago.

The tremble of performance, intimacy, secrecy, and desire on Lydia's face was immediate and strong. "Okay," said Amestoy, satisfied with the executive's shivering moans. "You were saying?"

Lydia dug her nails into the foam of her office chair. "Take her dress off," she said. "Please."

Corrine Amestoy gazed into Grace's eyes, enjoying the thrill of a new 'first-time' through the pleasure of woman on the screen. Then she undid Grace's clasp and pulled the white dress up over her blonde hair.

Grace's arms rose as she did it, revealing hairless armpits and a small-breasted figure of smooth, cream-white skin.

"Take her bra off," said Lydia, infatuated at the sight of Grace. "Hold her hard. Finger her. Push her panties aside."

Amestoy clicked Grace's white bra open, and it fell to the bed. The lawyer's small, pink nipples stood firm, and the captain teased her by stroking them—then grabbed ahold of her. In a gripped embrace, Amestoy slipped two fingers up inside her subject. Grace gasped and moaned, wet in her panties, as the captain massaged her vulva with dominant force.

Grace's eyes fell on Lydia's, and she bit her lip with excitement as she stared at the pleasure-filled woman in the office chair. "If you ever find me on Pleiana," Grace murmured, "you can take me. Just don't tell your husband."

Lydia breathed heavy, making tight circles against her clit. Then she paused, dropping her pants to the ground and pulling her panties down. From a spot behind her desk's recycling bin, she grabbed a think, pink, bullet-shaped vibrator. It buzzed as she laid it against her reddened vulva. "Do," she started, gasping as she whispered the words, "do you have a strap-on?"

Amestoy nodded, removing her hand from Grace to grab at the dildo and harness on the nightstand. "Tell me what you want, Lydia," she commanded. "If you want me to fuck her, tell me to fuck her."

"I want you to fuck her," said Lydia. "Hard. Keep the boots on."

Captain Amestoy looked at Grace with an anticipatory smile. "You heard the woman," said Amestoy, pulling her legs out of her undersuit and sliding the harness up. With a magnetic click, it cinched at her hips, its black belt riding up into her muscular ass and hugging her taint.

The dildo locked firmly into place. "We've never done that size," Grace whispered, sliding her panties to the floor. The go-go boots came up to her knees, and Amestoy touched the tops with her hand before slipping her fingers up toward her ass.

With a touch to Grace's vulva, Amestoy checked her wetness. It was more than enough to handle what was coming. "Lucky you," said the captain, and pounced on her with clutching missionary passion.

The grey dildo pushed deep inside Grace Burdette, spreading her pink lips and filling her as she squirmed. The holo-scanners whirred to adjust their framing, following the two naked women making love on the bed. Again, Amestoy kissed her, taking care not to thrust too fast as the petite woman took in the new size.

Then, as Grace growled with pleasure, Amestoy picked up her pace. She pushed hard and fast, pressing her palm to Grace's chest and knocking the air out of her with each grunting thrust. On the other side of the call, Lydia McNeil plunged her pink vibrator into herself, turning it up as she gritted her teeth and rocked against the seat. "Put," she panted, her throat vibrating with the tension of a woman close to ecstasy. "Put a finger in her ass."

The slight skip in Grace's voice as she heard the instruction was barely audible through her moans. Arching slightly back, Captain Amestoy placed her thumb in Grace's mouth, letting her suck on it as she pressed her tongue. "What does that taste like?" she asked.

"Cold sauna," Grace whispered with a breathy laugh, "and my pussy."

"Ready?" Amestoy asked, and Grace nodded. At this, the captain pressed her dry hand against Grace Burdette's throat and sternum, holding the woman down. Then she brought her wet hand lower, pushing Grace's legs apart and pressing a thumb against her tight asshole. All the while, she pumped against her, and after a rapturous moan from Grace she pushed the thumb inside.

"Oh fuck," Lydia half-shouted, her leg shaking in ecstatic bliss. Then she hushed herself as the orgasm pounded her. "Oh, fuck, Grace."

Captain Amestoy lingered, sliding deeper and shallower in Grace Burdette, listening to her quiet whimpers as she filled both holes. Then Amestoy pulled her hand and the strap-on away. "Come here," she said, patting the bed for Grace to nuzzle against her. The two lay on their backs now, right-way-up on the bed.

Amestoy took a ball-shaped massager from her nightstand drawer. Touching herself, she pushed its vibrating rubber up hard against her own clit as Grace cuddled her.

Slowly, Lydia McNeil came to her senses, watching the bronze, goddess-like woman pleasure herself with a worn-out damsel on her arm. Captain Amestoy looked over at the screen as the bliss-rent mother of two pulled her clothes back on. "Wish you were here," the captain said to her, "we could go for some peanut butter shakes once you made me come."

"Why peanut butter shakes?" Lydia laughed, spent.

"I dunno," said Amestoy. She adjusted herself, moving the ball-shaped massager down against her vulva. "I just feel like it." The control of the small machine in her hand was a comfort and a pleasure. "Our galley cook makes a mean one."

"Oh, you're on a ship?" said Lydia, chatty now in the flustered reality of what had just come over her. "I wouldn't have known, I mean. It's so nice. What's your line of work?"

"We're space pirates," said Amestoy, and howled as she came with the feeling of Grace against her hip.

"Mrs. McNeil?" a young woman's voice called from the other side. Lydia jumped up, and at once the line was hurriedly disconnected.

"Poor woman," said Amestoy, when her ears stopped ringing from the rush. "Looked like a fucking prison."

"You don't know that," said Grace. "Maybe it's exactly what she wants."

3 - PHYSICAL

Miles lay in his underwear on the seat of *Aurora's* medical examination table. Mia Rain was the sole medic on the crew, and as such the med bay was her exclusive scientific domain. Inside its gleaming white interior, a scanner in a white-plastic casing rotated above Miles, supplying a comprehensive picture of his health to a touch-screen display nearby.

At the screen, Mia Rain examined a heatmap of his body. Her hair was blonde and bobbed, like Grace Burdette's, but its layers had more natural goldenrod tones than the perfect bottle-shine of Grace's platinum. She had a bright, young face with a button nose, and rosy cheeks which twitched as she stared with great interest at her work.

She was also one of the only *Aurora* crew to regularly wear a uniform, donning her one-piece red-and-white medical jumpsuit on nearly every occasion. It was form-fitting, with a synthetic material that shined in the even med bay light.

"If you don't mind me asking," said Miles, after staring at her small butt and near-flat chest for some time. "How old are you?"

"Nineteen," said Mia, tapping a button which lifted him closer toward the sensor with a mechanical whirr. "That's older than you, operator."

"Nineteen?" said Miles. "Really? And how the hell are you a doctor? Pardon my language." The fatigue of his strange new ailment had weakened his manners, but he still felt the instinctual need to keep on good behavior around this young lady.

"I was a prodigy," said Mia, switching to a different type of scan. "I graduated medical school on Kaiten three years ago. Youngest ever to pass the exams. Then I had a falling out with my dad, I guess you could say. It was for the best. He made sure I lost my license, basically blacklisted me from my home planet. Corrine picked me up, and now I'm here."

It baffled Miles to hear someone on the crew call the captain by her first name, especially someone as young as Mia Rain. He wondered what exactly the relationship between them entailed. Then felt another pang of nausea, and his thoughts returned to his sudden sickness. "What is it?" he asked, pointing to the charts. "I mean, what's wrong with me?"

"Oh," said Mia, as if she'd forgotten about that portion of their conversation. "Radiation sickness. Fairly severe."

"Holy shit," said Miles.

"No, it's not surprising," said Mia, continuing in her blithe affect. "It's probably from when you and Corrine tethered down and got caught in that nuclear blast, right after you signed on."

"No, I know that," said Miles. "What I mean is, 'Holy shit, I have severe radiation poisoning.'"

"Don't be dramatic," said Mia. "It's not an issue. I've already made sure that your genome's compatible with our genetic cleanup. Almost everyone's is, unless you're a Volkji or a shapeshifter or something like that. I'll put you under, then I'll run it, then I'll give you an M5 chip for a week or so to handle the side effects. Wait. Do you want to be put under? Because it's always more fun for me to just numb the pain sensors and keep you awake."

"No," said Miles, "no, definitely put me under."

Almost before he knew it, he was awake again with two hours passed. "Carlotta?" he asked in a stupid haze, before he cleared that derelict word from his mind. He felt his back clammy against the operating bench, and looked down to see his flaccid dick exposed in the med bay air.

"Oh," said Mia Rain, following his gaze before handing him his underwear. "It was interfering with the cleanup scanner."

"Sure," said Miles, grunting as he slipped his underwear back on. "Well, I hope I was an enjoyable specimen, even unconscious."

"Oh yes," said Mia, "a wonderful sample."

Already, the nausea and pain in his chest was gone, but a new cold sensation had taken hold of the left side of his neck. He put his hand there, almost absent-mindedly, to find a metal chip about one-inch across implanted in his skin. "Fuck me," he said, tapping at the panel. "You're not making me a cyborg, are you?"

"You would *be* so lucky," scoffed Mia. "Don't monkey with that, you'll chafe. That's your M5 implant. It lets me monitor your vitals in the field. I can also use it to deliver hormones and stims into your bloodstream, to keep you level while you recover from the gene cleanup."

"Weird," said Miles, for lack of something better to say. "It's coming out after a week, though, right?"

"Sure," said Mia, "if you want. I haven't told you the fun

part, though. Just wait."

He heard the med bay door swoosh open, then turned to see her walk outside. She took another ten steps, passing the mess hall, and disappeared from view toward the front of the ship. "Where the fuck are you going?" he muttered, watching her leave.

"Nowhere far," came Mia Rain's disembodied voice through his spine.

Miles whipped around, looking for her. Of course, there was no person in the room. "I can transmit from my handset straight to the chip," she said, giving him chills as she spoke directly to his nervous system. "Voice is about the only thing it's rated for, nerve-wise, although I suppose I could try to give you a seizure with the right—"

"Voice is more than enough," said Miles. "Hang on, how can you hear me? Are you reading my brain waves?"

Mia Rain laughed as she walked back into the room, shutting off the transmitter on her handset. "No," she said, "I wish. Maybe one day. No, it's got a little microphone and a decent holo-sensor. I wouldn't be able to read a book in your hands, but I can see and hear the basics of your environment through the scan. For medical purposes, of course."

"Of course," said Miles, rolling his eyes at her. "Somehow I don't think this week can go by fast enough."

An evil, spider-like twinkle formed in Mia Rain's eye. "Well," she said, stepping closer to him, "if you're looking for ways to make the time go by, we could always play a little game."

"A game?" said Miles. "I'm a little busy for games."

"What about a wager?" said Mia. "A go-getter like you couldn't turn that down, especially a wager on your own abilities."

"My own abilities?" said Miles. "Which abilities?" He turned to sit up on the lab bench in his underwear, facing her square-on. *If I'm not careful, I'm gonna get hard in front of the doctor. Not that I think she'd mind.*

"Your ability to follow instruction," said Mia. "I like to call it Mia's Game. It's the best thing to do when you're stuck with an M5 chip in your neck, believe me. How it works is, throughout the week, I'll tell you a few things that I'd like you to do. If you do them all, you'll get a very sweet reward. If you don't, I get to use you for one of my experiments."

Miles stared into the orange freckles on her fair face. There was a light, irresistible playfulness in her eyes. "That is one of the stupidest proposals I've ever heard," he said. "I don't know what kind of idiot would ever write you a blank check for whatever maniacal behavior you'd ask 'em to partake in."

"And yet?"

"And yet," Miles said with a sigh, "I find it somehow intriguing."

"Because you're a man of action."

"I guess so," said Miles. "I mean, I guess we'll find out."

He extended a hand to shake, and Mia took it fervently. "Overconfidence," she said. "It's the uppers I just released into your blood with the M5. They cloud your decision making."

"What the fuck?" said Miles, and Mia had to talk him down as she laughed and laughed.

"No," she said, "no, I'm kidding. It's probably just your masculine stupidity—or my irresistible prodigy charm."

"Or some combination of the two," said Miles. Just then, his handset started to chirp from across the room with a four o'clock afternoon alarm. "Christ," he mused, considering his wager. "What have I gotten myself into?"

Mia Rain picked up Miles' handset, reading the alarm notification before dismissing it on his behalf. "Looks like you've gotten yourself into 'paperwork with Grace.' How fun."

"Yeah, it'll be a riot," said Miles, and stood to get himself dressed.

* * *

The air conditioning fan whirred quietly in the rafters of Captain Amestoy's cabin, cooling her tan skin as she lay with Grace. Beside her, the naked, well-fucked lawyer in the go-go boots sighed. Then she cleared her throat. "Why did you say that?" Grace asked. "That we're space pirates, I mean."

"Aren't we?" said Amestoy. She rolled to her side, facing Grace, and ran her fingers on woman's fair body. "We grab people off the street and fly away with 'em, just to make a few bucks. Only difference is, I guess we're pirates for the good guys."

"Good guys," said Grace, pawing at the massager in Amestoy's hand. "Maybe you could talk about some good guys while you finish me. Respectfully, ma'am."

Then a muffled alarm went off across the room. "Shit," said Grace, suddenly jolting up in her go-go boots. "KALI, what time is it?"

"Five past four," said KALI. "Operator Meyrich is in your office. I told him you may be delayed, but I didn't want to—"

"Fuck, I'm late for everything this week," muttered Grace, grabbing for her bra. "I've already cancelled on him twice. We still need to finish his paperwork."

Captain Amestoy grabbed Grace's bra and panties,

hiding them out of reach on a high shelf. "You want a good guy?" she asked. "There's one in your office. Go down there and finish up his paperwork. No bra, no panties. Show him what's on your mind. Then you can come up here and maybe I'll finish you."

* * *

Miles gnawed on the end of a pen while he waited in the chair across from Grace Burdette's desk. It was an ugly habit, but his oral fixation was not one easily broken. He hid the nibbled pen-tip as the door to the lawyer's office swooshed open behind him.

Grace looked like a mess. Her platinum hair was more than tousled, and her lips were stained with lipstick smears in a color she never wore. Her small breasts bounced beneath her dress, which fit a bit loosely on her thin frame, and Miles could see her hard nipples poking into the white cloth. As she sat, he swore he smelled a whiff of sex on her pale skin.

"Good afternoon," said Miles, hiding his surprise at her appearance. Whatever the hell was happening here, it wasn't his place to acknowledge it.

"Good afternoon, operator—"

"Miles, please."

"Miles," said Grace, with a fatigued smile. "Thank you so much for your flexibility."

She walked him through a set of documents, displaying each on a tablet which rested on her glass tabletop. First came the general liability form, followed by the specific liability exemptions for each of a dozen gruesome ways to die. Tax withholding came next, followed by an oath of loyalty to abide the republic's privateer code. It would have taken him five or six hours to read it all before he signed it.

With each document, Grace's legs spread, and with each

signature her short dress hiked a little further up toward her hips. Miles had to strain not to see it through the table's glass as he skimmed each page. Then she leaned forward until her breasts and pink nipples were visible through her deep dress neck.

"Gets a bit cooped up on a ship like this, doesn't it?" she said, staring at him with her chin rested on one hand. "Same people, same places. I don't know about you, but it's a far cry from planetside life for me."

Miles cleared his throat. "Maybe you could talk to Captain Amestoy about some shore leave," he suggested, not sure where to safely put his eyes. "You two are close, right?"

"Yeah," said Grace, "but I'm always up for making new friends, too."

The woman in front of Miles was fucking gorgeous. Her face and jaw were cut like a diamond, with elegant eyes and a body that was slim right up until it needed to be full. At the same time, he knew her relationship with Amestoy was locked-tight. Whatever 'do-not-fuck' list the captain had wanted to give him, Grace Burdette surely would have been item number one.

"Easy, cowboy," Mia Rain's voice came through his spine. "You're gonna pop a vein pushing that much blood straight into your dick. Especially over such an obvious trap, I mean, come on…"

Miles looked down at the retirement fund paperwork at the tablet. "Um," he said, struggling to say something that would make sense to both Mia and Grace, "can you tell me a little bit more about the context here, please?"

"Grace and Corrine do these fucked up little dares," said Mia, while Grace explained something about paycheck withholding. "It's best not to get wrapped up in it. At least, not like this. You'll just end up the fool."

"I see," said Miles, nodding. Whatever Grace had said about retirement accounts had been totally lost. *I don't know if I'll live long enough to have a retirement, anyway,* he thought. Then he signed and closed the last of the forms.

"So," said Grace Burdette, still looking him over like she could eat him whole. "Maybe some time you could tell me what it was like being a cadet at Elektra. I've always had a military interest, you could say."

Miles laughed politely, sliding his chair back. "That would be wonderful," he said. "But, unfortunately, Sergeant Maeslon's got my training schedule pretty packed these days. I'll let you know if that ever changes."

Grace looked a bit red-faced at his rebuff. "Of course," she said, straightening up.

"Bullet dodged, operator," Mia laughed through Miles' spine. "You've got more willpower than I would've expected. You might actually take me to the cleaners on our little game."

* * *

A few days went by without any more spinal messages from Mia Rain. "Are you watching me piss?" he said out loud one night at a second-floor urinal. Even though she gave no response, he had a lingering feeling that the answer was 'yes.' Once, he saw her in the hall, but she only passed with the aloof air of a cat that had no need to be pet.

"What's that?" his bunkmate Ana Sofia had asked him, seeing his chip reflect the light of her handheld video games in the dark. "New piercing?"

"It's to manage my recovery symptoms," said Miles. "Mia never gave you one of these?"

"I sit at the most mission-critical part of the ship," said the *Aurora* pilot. "If I'm ever badly injured, *hermano*, it means everyone else on this bucket is turbo-fucked."

By the fourth day with the M5 chip, Miles had not yet worked up the courage to jerk off under Mia Rain's often-derisive supervision. Still, he felt the urge building, and he knew he wouldn't make it a week without some kind of relief. It was with that feeling growing in his chest that he lined up for carne asada in the mess.

"Here you go, Operator," said galley cook Erik Hansen, giving Miles the same loving care he gave everyone as he piled up his plate with beef and rice. "When's then next chance we get to see you jump out of a spaceship? You were amazing the first time."

Miles chuckled at Erik's question, and his Norseman's lilt. "I'm still getting over the first time," he said, pointing to the M5 on his neck.

Plate and agua fresca in hand, Miles wandered to the galley's central island to grab a fork. The elegance of *Aurora's* shipboard dining never failed to impress him, especially after so many years eating barracks scraps as a republic cadet. Then a set of heel-clicks was followed by the familiar sound of Captain Amestoy making an announcement.

"Ladies and gentlemen," the captain said, drawing the eyes of the hungry, half-seated crew. She wore her dress uniform, pressed and buttoned. "Please, settle in. Consider this an informal mission briefing."

Miles looked around for a free spot at the mess hall tables. His first instinct was to slide in next to Ana Sofia, but rippling hunk Orson Buck was already taking up the rest of her bench. Then he heard a soft voice calling his name.

It was Engineer April Zamora, tattoo-sleeved and purple-haired in her orange flight pants and a stained white tank top. Miles knew of her in passing, remembering her mostly by her many facial piercings and association with the cyborg Evelyn Miyachi. Still, he was surprised that she knew his name, and more surprised still that she was calling him over.

Miles sat opposite the engineer. "I'm April," she said, fairly assuming that he might not remember. "Sorry, I just saw you looking for a place to sit, so I said 'hi.' I always hate that feeling, when it's like there's nobody I'd be comfortable sitting with, you know."

"Sure," said Miles, and noticed a plain-looking young woman with frizzy brown hair staring him down. She was seated next to April, and wore a surplus army jacket that brushed up against April's shoulder tattoo of a wyvern. "Hi," he said, to break her glare, "I'm Miles Meyrich."

"Oh, this is Nicki Stafford," said April. "She's our accountant."

"I still need your paperwork," said Nicki, barely smiling.

Miles took a sip of his agua fresca and murmured affirmative. "Yeah, I just signed them," he smiled. "Talk to Grace. I mean, to Miss Burdette."

"Gentlemen," Amestoy stressed, eyeing him as he realized the rest of the mess hall was silent. With a quick wave of apology, Miles turned to listen to the captain. "I just got off the line with republic command," she continued. "The good news is, we've got a pretty easy gig coming up. Five hundred grand, and all we've got to do is watch a VIP for one day in a controlled environment."

"Who is it?" asked Ana Sofia, eager.

The captain paused, as if considering whether or not to say. "Honeyblossom," she said at last, and a murmur spread across the mess hall.

"Am I the only one who doesn't know who this is?" Miles whispered to April.

"Oh, you know her," said April. "They've played her in like every space station concourse since June. Think of the song, 'Love Parallax.'"

The engineer hummed a few bars, and a faint memory of a glammed-out dance-pop tune returned to Miles' brain. "Right," he said. "Yeah, her. Cool, I guess."

"Captain, respectfully," said Erik, raising a hand from the galley in the back of the room. He was clearly geeking out to be talking about dance-pop on the clock. "Honeyblossom is performing at Blasted Edge Festival on New Canberra this weekend. Since we are on a course for the outworlds, ma'am, am I incorrect in guessing that this mission will also take place at Blasted Edge?"

"You are not incorrect," said Amestoy, to an excited murmur, "but that brings me to the bad news. I will not be granting any shore leave to attend the festival."

Ana Sofia whined the loudest of the half-dozen whiners in the mess hall. "But captain," she pleaded, batting doe eyes, "we've survived worse than a crowd full of college kids rolling on Red Jupiter. Think about the Tritian Maw."

"Yes, and I wouldn't grant you shore leave at the Tritian Maw, either," said Amestoy. "At the end of the day it's an outworld planet, no matter how many rich-kid midworlders they're flying in this weekend. I don't trust the newkies, and I don't trust the locals. Last thing I need is to pay fifty grand in a bribe to clear some weapons violation. Looking at you, Orson."

"Hey, he stays strapped for good reason," said Lex, then reached over for a fist-bump from Orson.

"Ma'am," said Ana Sofia, who at this point was sulking and may just have been looking for a fight. "I thought we didn't do private contracts. Don't tell me we're working for the newkies."

Miles decided to allow his ignorance on the subject of 'newkies' to remain for the moment, lest he be chided by the captain for speaking any further out of turn. "It's not private," said Amestoy, "and it's not the newkies, either. This contract comes straight from Lord Stahl."

At this new detail, Miles felt like he'd just found out that his favorite baseball player was his principal. "Wait," he said, half-standing in excitement. "*The* Lord Stahl? The one who held off the Silverthorne Horde during the Tung Chi Wa, then made a movie about it?"

Ana Sofia's derisive scoff revealed just how war-geek niche his interest was. "Okay," said the pilot, "so Honeyblossom herself is a non-starter for you, but you're excited about orders from some Colonel Dicklick?"

"That's enough, Serrano," said Amestoy, snapping her fingers. "Miles, since you clearly share my total lack of interest in the musical and vapid, I'm putting you on-mission."

"Bastard," Ana Sofia muttered, now more warmly teasing than genuinely mean.

"You too, Buck," said Amestoy, pointing to Orson. "Someone's gotta drag this kid outta the hot zone if he starts heaving in the field again."

"Oh, I'm good," said Miles, tapping his chip. It had turned in four days from a constant annoyance to a weird sort of cybernetic pride. "Mia's got me hopped up on so many drugs I could fight a bear."

"That's not true, for the record," Mia Rain announced from her table with XO Anwar. "He's just naturally stupid, and stupid brave."

Amestoy adjourned the informal meeting, and everyone resumed digging into their steak and rice. The whole time, Miles chatted with April and Nicki, watching their strange rapport as April rambled on and Nicki held back. Miles could see a strange twinge in the frizzy-haired accountant's face whenever Honeyblossom was mentioned, though he couldn't figure out quite why this may be.

"Hey," said April, nudging Miles across the table as the meal was ending. "Me and Nicki were gonna play some tennis after lunch. You should come."

"We have a tennis court?" Miles asked, shoving the last bit of rice onto his fork. "Sure, why not?"

4 - NEWKIES

Even after two weeks, there were still countless rooms and spaces on *Aurora* unexplored by Miles. In the gym, he donned his athletic-wear, then passed across the hall to a multi-purpose room with a clay-acrylic floor and a net across the middle.

Nicki Stafford and April Zamora were already engaged in a rally. Nicki wore a pastel polo top, while April was in an athletic top that showed off even more of the inky tattoos on her midriff. Both wore matching white tennis skirts and trainers, although the fit was quite different on April's skinny frame compared to Nicki's full hips.

"You play before?" April asked, after the rally ended and a round of re-introductions had passed.

"Sure," said Miles. "Some."

"I'll start you," said Nicki. Her hair was back in a curly brown ponytail, and her face had the character of a young woman you might see behind the counter at a deli, near the end of a long day's shift.

The muscle memory of casual games on the Elektra

fields came back quite quickly. Soon, Miles had a comfortable rally going with the accountant. He found himself having to hold back not to plant the ball outside her range of comfortable motion.

"Crush her," Mia Rain's voice came through his spine, nearly causing him to miss a save. "That's my next challenge." *How goddamn often is she watching me?*

Obliging, Miles took a breath and planted his feet. Then he delivered a sudden swing that sent Nicki chasing for a ball at the far back corner of her lines. "Maybe we should go two-on-one," April laughed, watching Nicki silently retrieve the ball from the back of the room.

Then the door opened, and Captain Amestoy entered in a white polo shirt and shorts. It was a far cry from the dress uniform she'd had on just prior. "Doubles," she said, pointing to four quadrants of the court. April and Nicki moved together, but she waved them apart. "You and me, Stafford," she said. "Meyrich and Zamora, take the far side."

April came over to Miles' side, nudging him with the black-inked image of a banshee on her elbow. "We can smoke 'em," she said, and he nodded polite agreement.

Over the next few sets, the two duos gave each other a fierce fight. Miles and Amestoy, diagonal on their respective rights, drove and returned shots with powerful impact. April and Nicki, meanwhile, traded swings as if wordlessly hashing out some deep-seated argument.

"I'd bet she'll be easy to work with," said Miles, remarking on the VIP of their upcoming mission during a break. "She's a professional just like anyone else, right? She can't have gotten where she is by making too many enemies."

"You'd be surprised," said Nicki. "About her, I mean."

Amestoy took a long pull from a canteen of water, then

offered some to Miles. He accepted, watching Nicki's face while he drank. "You know Honeyblossom?" he asked after wiping his mouth with the back of his hand.

"I used to," said Nicki, shrugging. "Back in school. We went to CYU together."

"Oh," said April, as if putting something very clean and obvious together for the first time. "Oh, is she the one?"

"Yeah," said Nicki, looking aside. Miles could tell the accountant didn't care for being the center of attention. At the same time, this story seemed mission-pertinent, and everyone in the room had a vested interest in her account. "Yeah, she was pretty awful."

"You guys dated, right?" said April. "For a little?"

"Not really," said Nicki. "I mean, it was something. I didn't know what I was doing. I felt a lot and, I don't know. She didn't want anyone to find out. I was still pretty much in the closet at that point. So was she. However much I was scared of coming out, it was like ten times worse for her. She was almost vicious about it. It's all so stupid. I won't get into it, but, basically someone saw us together, and the next day she freaked out and started telling everyone that I'd been stalking her and I was some kind of creep. She never even had anything against me, I don't think. She was just scared. But it really fucked me up for a while."

"Ouch," said Miles. "That really sucks, Nicki."

"Yeah, well," said Nicki, "I still wouldn't want her getting blown up, or whatever. So I guess it's good that Lord Stahl has us covering her this weekend."

Amestoy watched Nicki as the accountant put on a smile. Then April clicked her teeth and tapped her racket on the rec room wall. "She's in better hands with us than with the newkies," the outworlder engineer said.

"Okay, I keep hearing this word," said Miles, eager to

have a change of topic from the glum dregs of Nicki's college affairs.

"New Canberra Independent Authority," said Amestoy.

"Biggest pile of souped-up losers you'll find in this quadrant of the outworld," said April Zamora. "I'm pretty sure every shuttle-crashing dickweed from my high school ended up in the newkies after failing the S-SAT."

"You grew up on New Canberra?" asked the captain, turning her attention to the intercom on the wall. "KALI, why wasn't I briefed?"

"My records do not indicate Engineer Zamora's background," said KALI's mechanized voice. "My apologies. I will amend her personnel file."

"I left when I was sixteen," said April. "It's not exactly the kind of place you put on a résumé. Believe me, I was happy to leave for anywhere with a functioning republic legal system."

"Well, you're going back," said Amestoy. "You're a local connection, and it'll be good to have a reader on the ground if we're sniffing out threats."

"Hang on," said Miles, turning to April and with new eyes. "You're psyche-sensitive?"

Purple-haired April with the piercings and tennis top smiled. "You couldn't tell?" she laughed. "I've been reading you all day."

* * *

Ana Sofia straddled Orson Buck as she rode his cock. He sat in her pilot's chair on the bridge, arms on her hips and tactical belt around his ankles. Ahead, past the blinking lights of *Aurora's* flight controls, the glimmering, arid world of New Canberra glowed on the blackness of outworld space.

The pilot faced him, kneeling with her legs on either side of his hips. Her soft cotton shorts hung from one calf. Her pussy hugged him tight as she bounced up and down, touching her ass to his cool knees with each dip. Leaning forward, she twisted her hips back and forth, massaging her own g-spot with his huge dick as she moved.

She loved the sound of it. Orson leaned back, holding her thin waist as her round ass did its work. He had the perpetual, confident smile of a man who can coast through life without consequence. That look, and his muscular mid-thirties build, were a perpetual source of lust for the twenty-three-year-old pilot.

Ana Sofia tossed her straight brown hair backward, letting it fall against the back of her hoodie. Chin up, she moaned and squeezed her own tits through the fabric as she rode harder. "Come for me, *turro,*" she said.

"You first," said Orson, and adjusted his hips so his cock pressed hard against the top of her pussy.

"Oh," said Ana Sofia, surprised at the sudden rush of feeling. Dropping down onto him, she felt the orgasm rise, and steadied herself on the console behind her as it pulsed in waves.

Orson took over the thrusting motion, finishing himself inside her as she moaned and sighed. As he did, her hand slipped, and her palm pressed against the lock of some throttle control.

The whole ship shifted laterally. Ana Sofia could see a puff of RCS thrust off the starboard bay, and she could hear the surprised murmurs of the crewmen down the hall at the unexpected maneuver. "Plotting recompensation thrust to keep us within New Canberra orbital parameters," said KALI. "If your flight control action was intentional, Pilot Serrano, please inform me so I can cancel the correction."

Ana Sofia clenched against Orson, feeling his hot cum

fill her up. Then with one last shudder she slid off of him and to her feet.

A few drops of cum hit the floor of the bridge as she pulled up her shorts. The rest soaked into her underwear and shorts, creating small dark spot in the soft grey cotton. Kneeling down, she wiped up the drops with a clean service rag, then tossed it into the laundry chute.

Captain Amestoy entered *Aurora's* bridge abruptly, wearing her armor and carrying her helmet at her side. A slugdriver pistol sat on her suit's magnetic hip mount. "Don't think I don't know what you're doing in here," she said, catching a hint of Orson's pale, muscular hips and pubes as he hiked his black cargo pants up. "Nasty. Both of you. Just don't set off a missile, okay?"

"Enabling weapons control would take an… impressive string of mistaken presses," said KALI. "Nonetheless, Captain, I am taking appropriate precautions."

A 'thud' rattled *Aurora* as a drone-taxi shuttle docked with the bridge's airlock. "Your transit has arrived, captain," the navigational intelligence added.

"Thank you, KALI," said Amestoy, turning to see Miles and April in street clothes behind her. "No exo-suit?" she asked the operator.

"I made an operational choice based on the conditions in the field," said Miles, pointing to a borrowed graphic tee that read 'Sashimi Beats Music Collective.' "I'm blending in."

"That's Ropeburn's, isn't it?" said Amestoy. "I can tell by the beer smell."

"Even plainclothes, we're ready for anything," said April, pulling up her own shirt to reveal a concealed-carry pistol holster tucked into her pants. Her hair was half-slicked, and she looked just as likely to be some far-out rock musician as a festivalgoer. "After last time, I'm not screwing things up again."

"Wait, what happened last time?" asked Miles.

The airlock doors opened, and the four-seated drone-taxi beeped to announce its frustration with their dawdling. "Nothing," said April, "don't worry about it."

"Y'know, we could still put *Aurora* down in the festival district," said Ana Sofia, making one last appeal to her departing captain.

"Yeah, and have to keep tabs on everyone sneaking out to shows?" said Amestoy. "I don't think so. Plus, I'm not paying concert rates for some shitty New Canberra landing pad."

* * *

The drone-taxi dropped into the sunny New Canberra atmosphere with astonishing speed. "Holy shit," said Miles, watching the city center come into view below. "This approach vector would be so illegal at Elektra."

"That's everything here," said April. "Get used to it."

Across from Miles, Orson Buck cradled a compact rifle, which he'd folded over itself into a sort of lunchbox-shaped square. He wore his signature all-black, with sunglasses that reflected the glow of the outworld sun. Through the shades, it was hard to tell if he was asleep.

Beside him, Captain Amestoy flicked through the program for the day. "I don't know any of these people," she said, reading off names of pop acts and sim stars. "What happened to Gina Torani? What happened to Break Truth? Oh my god, am I out of touch?"

"Yes," said April, five years younger than the captain and reveling in it.

"Crazy that your friend knew Honeyblossom," said

Miles, seeing a ten-story hologram of the dazzling idol projected over Enterprise Square. "Nicki, I mean. I can't imagine."

"A pop star's just another name and a face," said Amestoy, nudging Miles' knee with her own. "I tapped you 'cause I thought you understood that. Don't get starstruck."

"Oh, I won't," said Miles. "Unless we run into Lord Stahl."

The taxi descended toward a docking area just to the north of Enterprise Square, near the festival gates. "Hey, taxi," said Amestoy, snapping her fingers to rouse the shuttle's intelligence. "We asked for a trip to sector C6. The Hotel Grandeaux."

"All travel within festival grounds is rerouted to the adjacent landing pads," a disgustingly cheerful male voice explained. "Please speak to an authority officer if you need any assistance."

With that, the taxi shuttle touched down, and its pod doors opened. Immediately, the smell of exhaust and orange blossoms filled Miles' nose. He'd only been to a handful of planets in his life, and each one so far possessed an incomparably different scent.

Amestoy only got a dozen steps past the pad before a pair of newkies stopped her. They wore ceramic armor painted baby blue and creamsicle yellow, polished with a wax finish that betrayed a total lack of combat exposure. Both were young men, probably in their mid-twenties, and carried a certain wily combativeness usually seen in mediocre cardsharks.

"Passes," said the gruffer newkie, extending a gloved hand.

"Republic privateers," said Amestoy, flashing her bounty license as she moved to step around him. To her shock, he shoved her back into place.

"Everyone needs a pass," said the suaver newkie. "Of course, they're all sold out, but maybe we can set you up."

"How much," said Miles, though he should have let the captain do the talking. Immediately, the two newkies seized on a possible mark.

"Two grand a piece," said the suaver one, and Amestoy balked in his face before he could finish. "That's good for all five days. You won't find a better deal than us."

"Something funny, beautiful?" said the gruffer one, scowling at Amestoy.

Amestoy had mind to deck him. Instead, she let her upper lip snarl and remained where she stood. "I didn't pay your shitty pad fees," she said, "and I'm not gonna pay for your shitty fake tickets either."

The two newkies exchanged glances, recalculating their game. Then the gruffer one switched on his shoulder-mounted scanner. It connected to a private database of faces and names, and after a moment a summary of Amestoy's past check-ins appeared on his wrist computer.

"Corrine?" he said, comparing her to the pixelated image on the wrist-computer screen. "You're a human wrecking ball, baby. I'm surprised they didn't flag you for crash insurance before you landed."

"As authority officers," the suaver one added, "it's within our rights to protect the public by blacklisting certain individuals from the city… if we feel it's prudent."

Orson sighed with the eyeroll of someone who'd been through this before. "I'm gonna get an iced tea," he said, pointing to a juice stand on the plaza.

"Stay where you are," said the gruffer newkie, snapping at the man with six inches of height and forty pounds of muscle on him. Arms crossed, the officer sized up Orson's folded-up rifle. "You're in a lotta trouble for just for bringing a piece like that out onto the plaza."

"Oh, fuck off," the captain muttered, and the newkies tensed. The whole time, Miles hung back as far as he could, catching April's eye as they watched Amestoy escalate and escalate.

"We're here on a favor for Lord Stahl," the captain continued. "I commend your little racket, and I'm sure you can pawn those tickets off on some unsuspecting mook before the day is out. But right now, unless you want the whole republic navy up your ass, you guys gotta see the bigger picture here and stand down."

"Listen, you dumb bitch—" the suave one began, and didn't have time finish before his face hit the pavement. His front tooth followed, separately, along with a spray of blood that arced from Amestoy's glove to the ground. In an instant the gruffer one drew his sidearm, training it on the captain's forehead.

Amestoy put up her hands, eyeing the man as if to dare him. On all corners of the plaza, Miles could see automated turrets turning themselves to face the four. If the newkies got pissed enough, he realized, he could be minced in a crossfire of lead real quick.

Then a woman in black put her hand on the standing newkie's shoulder. He jumped, twitchy, and with calm power the woman guided his gun back to its holster. On the ground, his partner coughed, stunned but still part-conscious.

Miles sized up this new woman. She looked about thirty-five, with black straight hair and thin liner on her monolids. Though she wore no insignia, everything about her screamed republic intelligence. "That's enough," she said, dismissing the standing newkie with a snakelike gaze.

Behind her, two festival medics loaded the downed officer onto a motorized stretcher.

"Ji-Yoon," said the captain, giving her a nod of respect. "You coulda showed up before I decked the guy."

"Let's get back into the shadows, Firewalker," said Ji-Yoon, guiding the four of them into a passage under the city monorail. "You need to be careful with that pneumatic fist, Corrine. If you kill a newkie in the middle of the street you might end up more trouble than you're worth."

"They're all dirty," said Amestoy. "And worse than that they're stupid." Miles kept close behind her now, eager to hear her back-and-forth with the mysterious woman. "If you want me doing favors for Stahl out here in raw space, you need to do your part keeping the local element off our backs."

"You're professionals," said Ji-Yoon. "You need to keep your cool."

Amestoy glanced back at Miles, who suddenly felt like he was eavesdropping. "Let's have this conversation another time," she said to Ji-Yoon. "I'm here. I've got a great team. This is Operator Meyrich. Specialist Buck. Engineer Zamora."

"Engineer?" said Ji-Yoon. "For a guard job?"

"She's a local," said Amestoy, conspicuously leaving out that she was a reader.

* * *

At the end of the tunnel, Ji-Yoon opened a mag-locked door, and the four found themselves in the lobby of the Hotel Grandeaux. Everything about it was decked in soft, resplendent color and design. While most of the festival grounds were loud and blaring, the hotel was carved into a lagoon-like retreat for the rich and sensitive.

An artificial river flowed outside, with sunbathers relaxing on inner tubes as the current carried them along. There was hardly a right angle in the entirety of the architecture. On the pool deck, music played from artificial rocks beside a shimmering waterfall. At the front desk, a line of sharply dressed attendants checked the midworld elite into their rooms and suites.

"Thirteenth floor, the Ambassador Suite," said Ji-Yoon, handing a pearl-colored keycard to Amestoy. Then she paused, giving the privateer captain a bizarre look that almost seemed to be pity. "I'll put in a call to authority control," she said, "so we can make sure they don't come at you with that bullshit with the local muscle again."

"Thanks," said the captain, pocketing the keycard. "You pick up anything on your net, go ahead and let us know, okay? We're all here doing the same job. Keeping people safe."

Ji-Yoon nodded, then disappeared back into the mag-locked passage. Orson and Amestoy walked ahead, with Amestoy's boots leaving deep impressions on the carpet as she crossed toward the elevators. Hanging back, Miles caught a quiet moment with wide-eyed April. "What is it?" he asked, smiling as he watched her smile.

"It's just," said April, turning the brightness in her face toward him. "I never thought I'd come in here. Growing up, you know. And if I did, I figured I'd be working the valet. Now look at us. I mean, I know it's just a job, but still. Here we are."

"Here we are," said Miles, taking her wonder in. "C'mon, or we'll miss the elevator."

5 - HONEYBLOSSOM

The elevator to the thirteenth floor was a glass cylinder. It rose from a fountain in the hotel's lobby, passing through the lobby ceiling to show off a wide panorama of the festival grounds as it climbed the side of the ornate tower. "Hey babe," said Orson, narrating a short video on his handset as he zoomed in on a stage where 'Saint Augustine' was performing. "Is that supposed to be someone famous or something?"

"You're playing with fire, Specialist," cautioned Amestoy, watching Orson snicker as he sent the teasing video off to Ana Sofia.

Following Orson and Amestoy down the hotel hall, with giddy April at his side, Miles got a strange sense he was on a field trip—or a family vacation. Not that he'd ever really been on either of those.

A smell of patchouli and pungent smoke hit his nose before they even reached the closed door of the Ambassador Suite. Despite her keycard, Amestoy knocked, and after a moment a skinny man with a beard and three loose necklaces opened the door. "Oh shit," he said, looking at Amestoy's red-and-black armor like she was Mars in human form. Then he put the pieces together in his head. "Honey," he called with a strung-out laugh, "your bodyguards are here."

A well-toned, lily-light woman's voice called back. "I only want one," she said, with the affect of someone who might spent all day reclined. "Tell that suit the rest have to wait outside."

The beard-and-necklaced man turned back to the privateers. His shirt hung open, and Miles watched him scratch at his hairy chest as he considered. "She only wants one," he said at last, as if they had not heard her.

"I'll take the suite," said the captain, making a plan in her mind. "You three take the roof."

"We don't need three units on the roof," said Orson, slapping his folded-up rifle. "I can lock it down just fine by myself, with the compact. Less conspicuous, too."

"Fine," said Amestoy. "Orson on the roof. If you're going solo, try to blend in a little. Buy a new shirt, something more like the kids."

Her gesture to Miles and April on 'kids' only reinforced Miles' upside-down image of a family vacation. "What about us?" he asked, checking the Featherhand pistol on his hip. "Lobby?"

"Negative on the lobby," said Amestoy. The whole time, the bearded man was watching them in a sort of half-dreamed stupor. "Meyrich, Zamora, go scout the area. Get the lay of the land and meet back here at nightfall."

"Scout the area," said Miles. "That sounds suspiciously similar to 'attend the Blasted Edge festival.'"

"Except you're sober and you're packing," said the captain. "And if I need you back here you'd better haul some major ass."

"Read and understood," said Miles. "Engineer Zamora, let's go do some reconnaissance."

* * *

Corrine Amestoy entered the Ambassador Suite of the Hotel Grandeaux alone. The bearded man shut the door behind her, humming some tune to himself as he tapped his foot. Compared to shipboard living, the suite was shockingly expansive. It ran as long as four rooms deep, with a huge floor-to-ceiling window letting in light at the farthest end. Other than that, the lamps were off, and the place was hazy and subdued.

Guitars, linens, and flashy clothes piled the floor, along with beanbags and half-eaten room service. Crossing a heavy bohemian rug, Amestoy pushed aside a draped white veil to see a huge, circular bed of white sheets and pillows.

Honeyblossom lay in the center of the bed, propped up on pillows which left her half reclining and half sitting. One hand lay above her head, as if she were posed for a magazine. Her trademark pink and gold body paint ran in thin lines down her ivory skin. In the haze and sunlight, atop the sheets, she looked as if were floating on a dish of milky-white face cream.

"You're not Ji-Yoon," she said to the woman in the red-and-black armor.

Amestoy looked her over. The pop star wore a silky robe, tied loosely enough to just barely cover her breasts and waist. She looked twenty-six or so, Nicki Stafford's age, and seemed used to having no one in her life ever seriously challenge her. She also looked plump and ready for the taking.

"No," said the captain, holding her helmet under one arm. "I'm not Ji-Yoon. I'm Corrine."

"Corrine," said Honeyblossom, sounding it out in a

wistful daze. Amestoy couldn't tell how lucid the woman was, but her eyes remained fixed on the armored privateer. "You're not a coreworlder. You're not really anyone, are you? Just a climber from, oh, maybe the Raskan Belt or somewhere dull like that. Speak some more, let me hear your accent."

"I've lived a lot of places," said Amestoy. "So has my accent. It won't tell you much."

"One of those muddy, in-between-worlds accents," Honeyblossom sighed. "A homeless accent, really."

Amestoy crossed the room, placing her helmet on a bookshelf at an angle where its front camera could observe the bed and the front door. "Mind if I leave this here?" she asked. "It's surveillance. Eyes and ears for my team."

"Oh, that's fine," said Honeyblossom. "Make yourself at home, poor creature. I'm going to call you 'poor creature,' alright? Would you like some food, poor creature?"

The captain said nothing as she settled into a chair against the suite's wall. A few books were scattered on the dining table, stories of foolish love and art and self-exploration on the road. Amestoy had no desire to pick up any of them. "I'm fine," she said at last, watching the bearded man take a hit of a half-burned joint. "Thank you."

* * *

Miles followed April Zamora through the crowds of the Blasted Edge festival. The sun was hot on the New Canberra pavement, and water cannons of various colors were employed to cool down the crowds. Everywhere they went, music pulsed through him, and every stage seemed to be host to a face or group he'd seen on some billboard or magazine.

"Never seen this many midworlders on NC," said April, shouting over the noise of a particularly bass-heavy track.

"There were always a handful. Old dudes looking for trouble, you know. Bachelorettes here to gamble and get smashed at The Palace. But not like this. I swear, I'd be hard pressed to find one *tongtin* in this crowd."

"Tongtin?" Miles shouted back.

"Local," said April. "Outworld slang I guess. All the stuff I tried to forget when I skipped town. Somehow it sticks with you."

She took his hand when the masses grew dense, pulling him through throngs of sweaty and half-dressed students from midworld universities. He could always find her shoulder by the slash-marks, spirits, and aurora tattooed on her skin.

"Did you get that when you signed on?" he asked her, when they'd found a shady spot to rest outside the flow of traffic. At her confusion, he touched his finger to the aurora borealis depicted on her tan shoulder.

"Oh," April smiled. "No, I didn't. I got it before, believe it or not. A year before."

"Is that part of being a reader?" said Miles, earnestly. "You see things before they happen?"

"God, I hope not," said April. "I don't think so, anyway. I'm not an oracle. I just get little feelings sometimes, you know."

"Like an oracle," teased Miles. "Well, what are you feeling now? Is some lunatic gonna try to blow up a pop star this weekend?"

She scrunched her face, twisting her thin lips and straight nose as she stared at him. Tucked between a lamppost and a wall, they were nearly nose to nose. "Not quite," she said, after thinking. "But something's going to happen."

The voice of a hollering outworlder dude broke the

moment. "Holy shit!" he bellowed in a heavy New Canberran accent, shirtless and tattooed with traditional runes on his buff, hairless chest. "April Lukpun Zamora!"

With a charge, he swept the woman into a wrestler's embrace. *If he'd been a terrorist, she'd never have had time to draw,* Miles thought with concern. *I guess that's why I'm here.*

April kissed the man's cheek and spoke a flurry of outworld slang that was too quick for Miles's ear to follow. "This is my friend Miles," she said, shoving Miles forward with excitement. "I mean, this is my colleague, Operator Meyrich."

"How's it going," said Miles, as the man brought him into a vigorous two-handed shake. It was all Miles could do to maintain a modicum of awkward professionalism in the face of this aggressive camaraderie.

"I'm Mele," said the shirtless dude. "I went to school with April maybe eight, nine years in a row. That's big for me 'cause that's all the school I ever did!" He gave an explosive laugh, then slapped April on the back. "Come on," he said, "I'm bartending at the end of the row. Everything's *midluk* prices, but I'll hook you up."

* * *

The pop-up bar was packed, with a line out the door. Tents shielded it from the sun, and huge misters poured cold water into heavy, oscillating fans. There was nowhere to sit at the counter.

Taking his place at the taps, Mele smacked his hand down in front of two half-unconscious dudes. "Time to go, guys," he said, assuming a put-on midworlder accent with astonishing quickness.

"Talking to me?" one of the guys slurred. Miles could see a CYU logo on his hoodie.

"Yeah," said Mele, leaning in. "I know you guys have

been doing lines of Jupiter off my bar counter. I bet you still got some on you, huh? That's two years in prison, *midluk*. Now get outta here before I call the newkies."

Sufficiently intimidated, the two college kids stumbled off, and Mele whistled for April and Miles to squeeze in. "I hate to be that girl, but we're not drinking," said April, leaning her bare elbows on the beer-tinged counter.

"Nah?" said Mele, honestly shocked. "You're not in one of those self-help cults, sister…"

"We're on duty," said Miles. He was surprised the man hadn't taken more notice of his sidearm.

"And you can't bend those rules none for old Mele?" the bartender smiled.

April looked to Miles, who shook his head. "Sorry, bro," she said, patting Mele's sun-worn bicep. "Maybe I'll catch you before we ship out. Then we can go hard like the old days."

Protesting no further, he served the privateers two tonics with lime, then got started on his backlog of heat-stricken customers.

Miles found it easy to stare at April Zamora. She had none of the characteristics of the hypothetical love of his life, or even the type of girl he ever would have noticed in class—not that there'd been many tattooed and purple-haired girls at Elektra in the first place. Still, there was an easy kindness to her, and a sort of natural empathy that flowed from her understanding smile as she sipped her drink.

"Speaking of pissing off newkies," she said, when the conversation had circled back around to Captain Amestoy. "This guy Mele once ran out of a bedroom butt-naked during a house party raid, just to tell the officers to eat his nuts."

"Christ," said Miles. "Then what?"

"Then he jumped out the window into the back of a garbage truck and rode it away."

"Bullshit," said Miles. "You're bullshitting me."

"He did!" said April. "Really."

"Wow," said Miles, laughing. "That's something."

She closed her eyes and put two fingers on his temple, breathing in. "Liar," she said after a moment. "You don't believe me."

"I do!" said Miles. "I do, I do believe. What is that? You're mind-reading me."

"Maybe a little."

"That's not cool," said Miles, laughing as he tapped at his M5 chip, "I do not approve. I've already got one load of trouble inside my head."

"Hi Miles," came Mia Rain's devilish voice through his spine. "I thought you'd forgotten about me." *Fuck me. I didn't think she could reach me from up in orbit.*

"What do you mean by that?" April asked, suddenly prying with delight.

"Nothing," said Miles. "Forget it. It's personal."

"No," said April. "No, I have a feeling I know exactly what you mean." With a turn of her head, she brushed her purple hair back, revealing a square neck mark where her own M5 chip had been recently implanted and removed. Then she leaned in to speak to the chip on Miles' neck. "Hi there, Mia."

"Kiss her," said Mia Rain's transmitted voice inside Miles' head.

"She's talking to you right now, isn't she?" said April. "I

don't even need to read you, I can see it in your eyes. You're a horrible liar, Operator Meyrich."

"Kiss her right now," said Mia, "or you're mine to dissect."

"Yeah," said Miles, wishing he could shut the chip up. "Yeah she is."

Then something new flashed in April's mind. "You didn't agree to that stupid game, did you?" she asked.

"I did," said Miles, presently resigned to his status as a horrible liar.

"And she's giving you orders right now?"

"Yeah."

April cocked her head a hair to the side, considering Miles Meyrich and the little voice inside his head. "Well, you better do it, then," she smiled.

Miles waited a breathless moment to think through what she'd said. *She's a mind reader, Miles. She knows everything already.* Then, with a delicate touch to her chin, her leaned in and kissed the lip-ringed girl at the counter of the pop-up bar.

It was a perfectly balanced kiss. Not anxiously quick, but not too lingering. Not a peck, but not too wet or deep or heavy. He pulled back, feeling the tingling after effects of her skin on his, and stared at her another moment longer. Then he laughed and finished off his half-warm lime and tonic. "I'm sorry," he said to April. "That was dumb. I shouldn't let the doc push me around."

"Oh, yes you should," said Mia Rain's voice inside his head.

April shrugged. "I get it," she said, "I'd hate for you to wash out of her game on my account. Plus, better me than Orson or Cap."

Miles imagined kissing each of the other two. Then he again remembered that April Zamora could read minds. "You'd end up like that toothless newkie if you tried anything on Amestoy," she joked. "Orson's your better bet. And even then, you'd incur the wrath of Ana Sofia."

"Heaven help me," said Miles. "She'd smother me in my sleep if she found out."

April's radio chirped through her handset. "Zamora," said Amestoy, sounding a bit impatient. "Can you get up to the hotel roof real quick? Orson needs help making heads or tails of some outworlder lookie-loo. Tell Miles he should stay in the field."

"Copy," said April, and put the handset away as Mele returned.

"Damn, you guys really are on duty," he said. He'd either missed the kiss, Miles thought, or he'd seen this kind of thing a million times before. "Well hey, lemme know if anything crazy happens. If you blow something up I wanna post it on my story."

"If we blow something up you better keep your ass back," said April, sliding off the barstool onto the slippery floor. "You shoulda seen what happened to Miles the other day. He got cooked."

Miles tipped generously, and April headed back toward the Hotel Grandeaux. "Mia," he said, as soon as he was alone in the crowd. "Listen, I'll do whatever you want, really, but please don't make a fool of me in front of the rest of the crew. I gotta live with these people for the next however-many years, y'know. I'm still trying to make a first impression."

For a moment, he was afraid she'd stepped away from her eavesdropping station in the med bay. Then he heard her voice come through again. "Careful what you wish for, Meyrich," she teased. "Go north toward that big white stage right now."

* * *

Miles followed Mia Rain's mysterious instructions, charting a path through the crowd toward a stage where "Guns of Minerva" was blasting on synth and guitar. As the music loudened, he felt more and more like he was walking into some sort of trouble.

"Stop here," said Mia, when he was a few feet from the side of the show's front railing. It had taken a lot of shoving and negotiating to get this far. "Do you see a girl on your left in white?"

Oh no. Miles turned to his left to see a girl in high-waisted jeans and a white tube top dancing with her friends. She had a strong jaw, with blush and foundation well-applied on a pretty-if-typical undergrad face. Her bust bounced in time as she jumped up and down, belting the words. "Yeah," he said. "I see her."

"Go up to her and say what I say," said Mia. "That's your next order."

Miles approached, heart pounding from the sheer stupidity of the act. She was the kind of girl he wouldn't have the guts to talk to even after four beers at an Elektra home game. "Hey," he said, and then realized that Mia had not yet given him instruction. Already, he was jumping the gun.

"Hey," said the girl, with a tone right on the precipice of interest and annoyance. That was already a warmer reception than Miles had expected. "I like your shirt."

Miles had to look down to remember which band was on the shirt he'd pilfered from Ropeburn. "Sashimi Beats, yeah, they're fire."

"Ask her if she's here with her friends," said Mia Rain.

"You here with your friends?" he asked, although that much was pretty obvious.

"I just know them," said the girl. "They're all pledge sisters, but I'm not."

"Okay, you're in," said Mia. "Ask if her she'd fuck you right there against the railing."

Oh Jesus. Miles visibly winced, no doubt to the girl's confusion. This next move, he realized, was like diving into Elektra's ice-cold lake on a January morning. It was better to do it whole and fast than tip-toe your way in. "Hey," he said, trying a laugh as if it was a passing thought. "Would you fuck me right now against the railing?"

The girl laughed. Laughing was a good sign. It was better than an Amestoy-style punch. She looked him up and down, eyeing his muscular forearms and lean athlete's build. Then a tall, lanky guy in glasses came up beside her.

The lanky guy was her age, with patchy buzzed hair and a spotty complexion. Funny enough, he was also wearing a Sashimi Beats graphic tee. "You need to fuck off," he said to Miles, driven by liquid courage and a total absence of charisma.

For a second, Miles was ready to fight this guy. It was absurd to be challenged by someone so slovenly, and more absurd to back down right away. At Elektra, it would have been his honorable duty to pound this guy into the mud. Then he remembered this wasn't a military school. He had no real interest in the tube-topped girl, and he definitely didn't want to start a brawl while on assignment. "Peace," he said, and smiled again at the girl before slipping back into the crowd.

"Wait!" said Mia, stopping him mid-step.

"I'm not gonna fight him for you," said Miles.

"No, no, forget that dweeb," said Mia Rain. "Look to

your right, further down, on the rail. Black skinny jeans. Leather jacket. She looks like a wild ride."

Miles saw her. He wasn't sure how this girl wasn't cooking to death in the New Canberra sun. *Maybe she's a local,* he thought, judging by her style and skin tone. With polite taps to strangers' backs, he slipped forward, joining her right as the next song kicked off.

This 'girl' was probably thirty. She had a frank face, with a small, wide nose and pocks from old acne scars on her orange-bronze complexion. Her lips were bright red, and her brows were lined above her deep brown eyes. She was short, much shorter than Miles, and her full cleavage squeezed between the open lapels of her biker jacket.

"Tell her your name is Tolstoy," said Mia, and he could hear a giggle in her tone. "Tell her you're a stereo system repairman."

"Hey," said Miles, going for broke with no expectation of success. "I'm Tolstoy. I do shipboard electronics engineering."

He was pretty sure she couldn't hear a word he'd said over the roaring guitar. "Yolanda," she said in a New Canberran accent. Then she took his hand to shake. "You're a pretty boy."

"You know, that's funny," said Miles, "that's what my roommate calls me, too."

"Go, go, go," said Mia, with the authority of a dispatcher sending in a SWAT team. "You're in. Do it now."

Miles smiled and blushed. "Listen," he said, almost feeling bad for annoying this sweet woman. He decided to pose his question as a more relaxed hypothetical. "Would you fuck a guy right here on this railing? Would you fuck me?"

Yolanda glanced around, looking for he-didn't-know-what. Then moved closer and pointed to a portable bathroom just past the crowd. "I'd fuck you in there," she said.

"The toilet?" said Miles. He paused, waiting for some kind of command from Mia Rain. Then his four jerkless days of pent-up arousal took control. "Let's go."

Miles led the woman in the biker jacket out of the stage's festival crowd. The walk away from the stage felt surprisingly casual, almost typical, except for the fact that he had some strange woman twelve years his elder holding his arm.

Luckily, there were more stalls than people needing to go. Choosing the green plastic toilet at the end, he took a moment to scan for nosy pedestrians before going in. There were no newkies in sight, and none of the festivalgoers nearby gave one shit about him. This was the furthest, most barren end of the festival, and nobody except a few food trucks seemed to be operating with any real authority. "C'mere," he said, guiding her into the stall. "C'mere, with me."

6 - TAKEN

April Zamora took the elevator up to the fourteenth floor of the hotel, a rotating lounge and restaurant currently closed for renovation. Then she took the emergency stairs one flight up to the roof. "Hey," said Orson Buck, sitting in a folding camp chair five feet away from the edge. At the captain's order, he'd replaced his black tee with a banana-printed tropical button-down shirt.

On his right was his unfolded compact rifle, resting on the ground with its bipod out and digital sights engaged. On his left, he held a scrappy outworld man by the scruff of his t-shirt.

"You look good!" said April, laughing as she saw his new outfit. "You should wear more colors, Orson."

"Thanks," said Orson, sunbaked and irritable. He pushed down on the lanky outworlder's shoulder, forcing him into a kneeling position. Then he pulled a telescoping camera from the man's bag. "Found this skeezer hanging off a window-washing drone, tryna snap pictures of our VIP indisposed through the suite window."

"Paparazzi?" said April, watching the man's shiny,

bronze face contort in fear as Orson manhandled him. "There's gotta be a hundred out here."

"Not a pap," said Orson. Then he tossed April a journal from the outworlder's bag.

The purple-haired engineer flipped it open. Then a chill cut down her spine as she looked at the pages. Inside, dozens upon dozens of drawings depicted the face and body of Honeyblossom. They were rough, but the shape of her hair and body paint were clear enough.

Almost all the sketches were depraved. Some seemed drawn from magazines or leaks, with Honeyblossom posed nude in her apartment or on a music video set. Most were more imaginative, with cocks, microphones, guns, and broom handles penetrating the pop singer in every hole. Past those, the scenes turned violent, with arms or limbs sawn off as the woman hung in chained-up sexual imprisonment.

April felt nauseous, and soon gave the book back to Orson. The act of guarding the entertainer now seemed much more essential than before. "He's been spouting off in that dumb desert-speak since I grabbed him," said Orson. "I thought maybe the two of you could have a heart-to-heart."

April felt her hackles go up when she heard him say it. "I can tell you're stressed, so I'll let it go," she said, "but maybe don't talk shit about my home planet while you're asking for my help."

"I'm sorry," said Orson, and to her surprise looked genuinely contrite. "My bad."

Approaching the man, April put her fingers on the sweat-slicked temples of her fellow outworlder. *"Sabaidi ai,"* she said, and spoke a few more guiding words to him in the New Canberran pidgin as she probed his thoughts.

Past the fear and self-preservation, a deep well of dark fixation swirled. In his mind, she could see him playing with a knife, cutting his own skin and the cover of a magazine where Honyblossom's face smiled up. Then she saw him turn the blade on a store mannequin dressed in the singer's hair and wardrobe, carving deep notches into her face.

She didn't need or want to see anything else. "He's dangerous," she said, letting go as the man shut his eyes and started to cry. Such outbursts were common among people with dark secrets, when a reader probed their inner mind.

"Do you think he's the one Ji-Yoon warned us about?" Orson asked, then elaborated when April's face was blank. "The fed told us there was net activity about a possible lone wolf attack on Honeyblossom this weekend. That's why Stahl has us out here. He'd rather not have troops on the ground in outworld space, but he doesn't trust the newkies to handle VIPs."

"I wouldn't know," said April. "But you shouldn't let him near that woman. Ever."

Orson flipped through the journal again. "I think he's the guy," said the specialist. "He fits every part of the profile, except for the weapons experience. And I know for a fact those intel suits can't nail a profile for shit."

A newkie patrol shuttle soon set down on the roof. "I called you guys half an hour ago," Orson griped. "I've got a perp here you can book on trespassing, breaking and entering, whatever else you want to throw in there. Just keep him locked up until our VIP's off world."

The lead officer glared at Orson as he cuffed the stalker. "You're lucky daddy fed is here to watch your ass," he hissed at the privateer specialist. "On any other day, we'd give you a real rough ride after what your bitch captain did."

April shivered at the threat, but Orson was beyond unphased. "Get outta here before I throw your dumb ass off this roof, newkie," he laughed. "You dipshits talk like you're in some gangster flick. I've seen better rackets run by middle schoolers."

April stayed silent until the shuttle departed, leaving the two *Aurora* crew alone. Then she gave an astonished chuckle. "Holy shit," she said to the huge man in the banana-patterned shirt. "I think every kid who ever grew up in The Stacks would crown you king of the hood if they saw the way you handled those newkies."

Orson shrugged. "You just gotta show 'em they can't push you around," he said.

"Maybe," said April. "But it helps to be a rich, six-two offworlder with gun and a fed connection."

Orson nodded. The he raised his handset to radio Amestoy. "Boss," he said, "just nabbed our probable alpha-threat and delivered him to impound. We should keep eyes up, but I think we're gonna be in for a quiet rest of the night."

"Copy," Amestoy's voice came back. "Good work, Specialist."

* * *

Miles locked the plastic door of the portable toilet, squeezing his body up against the stranger in the leather jacket. The stall was, thankfully, an upgrade from those that Miles had been subjected to as a kid. Instead of an open pit, a closed and sealed lid covered the seat itself. Instead of a fecal smell, the scent of disinfectant and fan-regulated air filled the stall. What hadn't changed was the warm green walls, or the tan roof that soaked up the heat of the sun overhead.

Miles pushed Yolanda against the wall, kissing her on her thick crimson lips. She smelled salty, with a strong hint of artificial rose perfume. Running his fingers through her black hair, he realized it was unlike any texture of hair he had felt before. It was coarser, with a dryness that ran until it reached the sweat of her scalp. He wondered how much of that texture came from the hairspray she had used to give it its shape.

The woman was hungrier for him than anyone he'd ever known, with the possible exception of Elektra's Dean Marian. Since his first foray into penetrative sex with Carlotta Tora two weeks prior, Miles felt like the floodgates of lust and conquest had opened for him with his commission on *Aurora*. He was young, he was hungry, and he was ready to take as much from the world as it had to give.

"You're a hot thing," said Miles, grabbing at her breasts under her jacket as he held her. Then he reached behind her back and undid her bra clasp. It fell to the floor, and Miles breathed in a big whiff of her chemical hairspray as he felt her up. Her nipples were big and firm, and her tits were larger than any he had felt before.

"You want me?" she said softly, touching his ear. It was clear that she found him equal parts fuckable and cute. "You want a *tongtin* mama?"

"Oh yeah," said Miles, kissing from her ear down to her collarbone. Then he knelt and held her as he sucked on her dark nipple. She stuffed her small-fingered hand down her own jeans, moaning as he licked and kissed. "Oh yeah, I want you."

"I want you, too," Yolanda whispered, bringing him to his feet. Then she dropped to her knees and pulled at his belt buckle. "I want you in my throat, pretty boy."

She pushed Miles' hands away as he tried to help. Clearly, she relished doing the work of opening this package. With his belt open, she unfixed the button of his jeans, then pulled the zipper to the hilt. His dick throbbed through his white briefs as she exposed them, and he hoped that he wouldn't come too quickly as she went to work.

She slipped his dick out through the flap of his briefs. It lay straight and hard, spanning eight solid inches until its tip touched the woman's lips. "Big boy," she smiled, impressed and surprised as she looked him over. Then, with a metal piercing on her tongue, she pushed forward and took his hard cock in her warm, wet mouth.

Miles leaned back with a moan, listening to the music that shook the green plastic walls. He thought he might actually know this band, for once, as the pleasure took him in.

"Not a bad service weapon, Meyrich," said Mia Rain through his spine. For one blissful moment he'd forgotten she was there. "I was wondering how long I would have to wait to appraise it at full mast."

He almost responded, before remembering that Yolanda could still hear him. Instead of engaging with the girl in his head, he lay his hand on the back of the outworld woman's skull and watched her take him deep into her throat. It made the strangest sound, almost a wet choking, but the lust in her eyes removed any doubt that she enjoyed it.

Then she pulled away. With a smile, she gripped his dick one-handed and pushed it upward, sucking on his balls. He hadn't even faintly understood what pleasure could come from it, until he'd felt it here. "Oh, Christ," he moaned, almost stumbling as she stroked his cock while continuing to suck. "Yolanda, you're gonna make me cum."

At that, she paused, smiling with satisfaction as she looked at the strapping young man reduced to a pleasure-strewn mess. "Fuck me here," he said, pulling her black skinny jeans and lacy panties down as she turned around.

"Meyrich, your scans are *bad*," said Mia Rain. "You're gonna cum in three seconds if you don't settle down.

Because I'm a sweetheart, I'm gonna hold your orgasm response back a little. You do a good job on her, and you can get a little something for yourself."

Fuck off, space witch, and let me cum already. Miles grumbled as she spoke the words. Then he felt what it meant to be 'held back' a little bit. He leaned forward, taking hold of Yolanda's full tits with two hands as she stood on the lip of the bathroom moulding for height. With a kiss to her temple, where her black hair became glistening cheek, he pushed his slicked cock up inside of her.

He was permanently on the edge of coming, but not there. Driven to a fit of furious lust by this feeling, Miles pounded and pounded against the woman in the biker jacket. *"Luksai,"* she said, getting louder in her moans as he slammed her and the bathroom wall shook. "Use me, use me, oh!"

After six minutes, almost out of nowhere, Yolanda came with a shriek. Miles kept at it, putting a hand under her neck to squeeze her jaw as his hipbones bounced on her full ass. Then his own release finally arrived. With a grunt, Miles took her by both hips, slamming himself up into her as far as he could go. Then he filled her brown pussy with four days worth of cum.

Insatiable, Yolanda dropped to her knees again, sucking and licking him clean as he shivered with feeling. Then a loud banging rattled the toilet's locked door.

"Just a second!" said Miles.

"Yolanda!" a low outworlder man's voice bellowed back. "I know you're in there you fucking whore! Bring your boyfriend out, I'll beat his ass!"

"Oh fuck," Mia said through the implant. That had been his first thought as well. He stuffed his dick back into his pants, watching Yolanda hurry to pull her own black jeans and panties up. She left the bra behind on the bathroom floor.

Miles drew his sidearm and held it at his side. "There's no Yolanda here, man," he shouted. "You got the wrong stall. I'm just taking a shit."

He heard a mutter, then the sound of footsteps retreating. Standing still, he unlatched the safety on his pistol. Then he saw Yolanda eyeing the weapon with a little too much interest. "Stay back," he warned her, more from preemptive fear than anything else. "Don't try anything on me."

Then there was the sound of a heavy engine's roar. At once, the bathroom stall was knocked to its side, shoved by the front grill of an SUV. The lid flew off, and the walls broke into three modular pieces as Miles flew, stunned and bruised, onto the festival dirt.

His pistol scattered out of his hands. "Miles!" Mia shouted as he reached out to grab it. Before he could, two men in leather jackets and boots heaved him off of the ground. Miles balled groped at the air in rage, turning to prepare for hand-to-hand combat. Then he felt a machine gun barrel press into his belly.

"Throw him in the trunk," a guy in his late thirties said, sizing up stunned and ragged Miles. All of them wore matching black leather jackets in the same basic style as Yolanda's.

"Miles!" Mia shouted again, but there was nothing she could do as he was tossed in the back with a bulletproof lid on top of him. In darkness, he tried to regain his senses as he heard the leader yelling at Yolanda.

"Boss, newkies," another of the gangsters said, and a moment later the SUV was driving on the dirt field again.

Miles grabbed for his handset, but it was gone. The only piece of tech on his body was the chip in his neck. "Mia," he croaked, coughing up dust. "Help."

"Shut up, cunt," a leather-clad goon barked at him, banging on the wall that separated him from the passenger section of the SUV.

"I'm with you, Miles," said Mia. "We'll get you out. Just hang on. And please don't let anything happen to that chip."

7 - HANNAH DUNN

Captain Amestoy was in her third hour of staking out Honeyblossom's suite. In that time, the pop star had taken a forty-minute shower, had her body paint re-done, called her manager to whine for another half hour, fallen asleep, and woken up without remembering why Amestoy was there. "Oh right," she said after some confusion, "you're the poor creature they've given me as a guard dog."

Shortly after that, KALI came through the captain's line on the emergency band. "Status," said Amestoy, stepping into the bathroom for a modicum of privacy.

"Green," said KALI, speaking through the wrist computer of the captain's suit. "However, there has been a development with Operator Meyrich. He's been... kidnapped."

"Fuck me," Amestoy groaned. "Pirates?"

"Miss Rain believes it's some sort of local gang," said KALI. "His vitals are stable, and she's monitoring his situation personally. I am not privy to the data."

"Does she have a location?"

"She's working on it. I have suggested we dispatch enforcers Rockbridge and Avar in *Sanpi,* so they can assist in the rescue."

"They're gonna fuck us on the parking fees for that shuttle," Amestoy grumbled. Two hours of Honeyblossom had put her in what was perhaps an unduly unsympathetic mood. "Fine, load Lex and Joe in the shuttle and keep 'em on standby. They can broadcast the bounty clearance if they need to do a hot approach into the city. Let's just try not to piss off the newkies too much if we can help it. Oh, and put XO Anwar in charge of the extraction. I trust Mia, but she's not an operations girl."

"Understood," said KALI.

Amestoy walked out of the Ambassador Suite bathroom, to Honeyblossom's curious eyes at the head of her circle-shaped bed. The woman was back in her loosely-tied robe, and had perked up at the sound of the radio conversation. "Drama?" she asked, pointing to Amestoy's wrist computer.

"It's not about you," said the captain. "I'm handling it."

The beard-and-necklaced man had long since wandered off to some other floor. Alone, Honeyblossom played with the snaps of her costume jewelry, until a new voice came in over her rose-colored handset. "Honey," said her middle-aged manager, using the name that all of her inner circle used. The way this man said it, however, was more sober and more hollow than the others.

"Yes, Bertie," said Honeyblossom, staring again at Amestoy.

"Those, uh, those boys you met at the club set the other night are here," said Bertie. "Well, the one, and the other one he mentioned."

"Oh, send them in," said Honeyblossom, and a few

minutes later the front door clicked unlocked.

The boys were maybe nineteen, dressed in the casual style of midworld festivalgoers. They were tall, thin and strong like Miles Meyrich, but possessed a sort of awkward immaturity below their years. *Or, perhaps they're typical for their years, and Miles is just inordinately confident,* Amestoy mused.

Honeyblossom pulled her robe tighter around herself, sitting up as they stood in the entryway. She did not make any motion to leave the bed, or draw them closer. "Right," said the singer, as if recalling a very distant night ten years ago. "The one with the nice eyes."

The taller boy smiled, bashful, at the remark. "Alex," he said. "And this is my buddy, Toshi. The one you saw on my feed and said to bring."

"To-shi," said the singer. "How wonderful. Please, come here. No, slower. Yes. On your knees. Crawl. That's good."

On their hands and knees, the two boys crawled at a snail's pace toward the woman. The whole time, she reclined in her body paint, beckoning with little flicks for them to come nearer or pause.

Corrine Amestoy adjusted in her seat, causing it to creak under her heavy armor. The dark-haired boy, evidently Toshi, glanced over at the privateer with a nervous smile from his position at the foot of the bed. Amestoy gave no reaction.

Slowly, Honeyblossom extended one bare foot toward Alex's face. Gently, he rested it against his cheek, then began to touch it as he kissed her painted toes. "Lick it," she said, and he began to slide his tongue along her freshly washed and moisturized sole.

Toshi, meanwhile, sat on his knees. After a moment, the singer sat up on the edge of the bed, with one of the young boys kneeling at each of her knees. With two hands, she cradled Toshi's face, examining his cross-country runner's neck and jaw. Amestoy could see his Adam's apple bounce as he swallowed.

"You're beautiful," Honeyblossom told him, almost crooning. "You're a beautiful little piece of coral. Go wait at the table over there with that poor creature."

Amestoy saw Toshi blink with confusion, though she was not sure which part had tripped him up. Then, rising, the boy walked over to the suite's side table and sat opposite the captain. "Hi," he said, giving her an awkward wave.

The captain glanced at her helmet, still sitting where she placed it on the bookshelf, then returned her attention to the bed. The singer had instructed young Alex to strip, and he'd taken the shirt and ripped jeans off of his muscled figure. For his shoes and socks, he had sat on the floor, and when at last his underwear came off he removed it with his back to Toshi.

"Crawl up to me," said the singer at last, staring at the boy's freshly shaved pubes and hard, pink dick. "Slowly, inch-by-inch. Hug the bed."

As she instructed, the boy made a painstakingly slow crawl up from the side of the bed. Honeyblossom lay back, and with each small advance he made he took time to kiss and caress the next highest part of her leg.

Eventually, he reached the place where her robe covered her hips. Like parting the petals of a flower, the singer slipped her silk robe's hems aside. Beneath, a waxed and flawless vulva glistened like a honeydew.

"Make love to it," she told him, guiding his head slowly down until he was kissing her pussy lips. "Like it's your sweetheart. Make out with it. Be tender."

Nervous but eager, Alex began to eat her out, resting his hands on the pink and gold stripes on her legs. "Watch the paint," she said, guiding his hands further out before sprawling in an idle daze.

Amestoy looked at Toshi, who couldn't decide whether or not to watch. "You guys fuck?" she asked him, pointing to Alex's ass.

"Huh?" said Toshi, who seemed to be in the middle of an out-of-body experience. "No, we just run track together. I don't know him that well."

"You're a Honeyblossom fan, though?" she asked.

Toshi shrugged in his t-shirt and brand new hypebeast jacket. "I guess," he said. "I'm mostly here for the underground stuff. I just came here as a favor."

A call came in on Honeyblossom's handset, and she took it. "Keep going," she told Alex, before hushing to a murmur on the phone. "Hey Bertie. Yeah they're still here. No, just the one. I just wanted to see the other one. Yeah, he can watch. Maybe I can have them do each other."

Toshi fidgeted in his seat, looking to the fading sun and the concerts outside. After another moment, Amestoy leaned in. "Y'know, you don't have to stay here for this," she told him. "If it's not your scene, kid, just leave. There's no shame."

The singer sat up against the pillows to look at her bodyguard. "What was that, creature?" she asked, pulling Alex closer so he could continue to eat her out at this new angle.

"I said the kid can do whatever he wants," said Amestoy. "He can leave."

Now Honeyblossom pushed young Alex away. "And who are *you*," she said in her ethereal lilt, which now possessed a cutting undercurrent, "to say anything about *my* affairs?"

Amestoy cracked open a mini water bottle from the table and took a drink. "I was just making conversation," she said, measured in her tone as she met the singer's glare.

"Well, next time, try being seen and not heard, you spacer mutt," said Honeyblossom.

"Okay, junkie," said Amestoy.

What the *fuck?*" said the singer, too astonished to even be angry right away.

The captain shrugged. "If you wanna square up, Honey, let's go," she said. "I don't know who you're used to, but I'm not gonna sit here and take it when you kick me. Even if I have heard worse from dumber jupe-heads than you."

"Excuse me?"

"Look at your fuckin' nose," said Amestoy. All the disdain and frustration of the afternoon was rolling out. "They've got you on so much glitter in here, I'm surprised you can walk straight. Why's that, huh? So they can keep you from seeing what a cell you're in?"

Alex was standing now, holding his jeans, unsure of whether or not to start getting dressed. Leaning forward on the bed, Honeyblossom spat fury at the captain. "Get out."

"No," said Amestoy.

The singer didn't seem to understand what this word meant. "I said get out," she repeated, stumbling in her tone from the shock of unexpected conflict.

"No," the captain repeated.

"*You!*" the singer roared, turning her attention to the two people in the room she could control. "Boys, get out!" Now Alex was racing to get his shirt on. "No changing, just go! Take your clothes!"

Driven out by this body-painted she-devil, Toshi

scrambled into the hall. Alex's semi-soft dick flapped behind as he followed, bottomless and panting. The door fell shut behind them, and Captain Amestoy was alone in the suite with the singer in the silken robe.

Honeyblossom seethed, flexing her nails like claws at the ends of her fingers as she took steps toward the power-suited privateer. "You trash," she spat. "They're going to blacklist you from every civilized sector. There won't be one club, one hotel in the galaxy that doesn't spit your money back out in your face."

"Is that all you know about the world?" Amestoy asked, genuinely amazed by the warped human being before her. "Hotels, clubs, and money? Your life is a mirage. It's been one ever since you stopped being Hannah Dunn."

Amestoy knew how hard the singer had tried to bury her legal name. She knew exactly how it would land for her to hear it. Honeyblossom paused, unsteady, searching the face of the black-haired woman in the armor. "It's better than yours," she sneered. "Oil and grime and recycled air. I'd rather take a bullet through the head than live like you mercs do."

"Oh, what you wouldn't give to live like I do," the captain laughed. Now it was her turn to take a step forward, watching the singer shake with anger in her silk robe. "How long has it been since you've been with a woman?" she asked. "How long have you spent yearning for what you're afraid of?"

The change in pallor and expression on Honeyblossom's face was immediate. "You're delusional," she said, but the words came shaky now. "You fucking wish."

"I don't have to wish," said Amestoy. "Just like Nicki Stafford didn't have to wish."

Another blow to the singer's façade left her reeling. She stood still, unable to form a sentence, as Amestoy neared to a single foot of distance. "Now," said the captain, "you can call old Bertie and have the newkies drag me outta here… or you can leave those boys behind and let me kiss you like you should be kissed."

There was a lonely young woman's face underneath the face paint and the glittering makeup. Her fair hair was wispy in the breeze of the suite's central air, and she choked as she tried to find the words in her head. "K-kiss me," she said, almost as a question but not quite.

Captain Amestoy took Honeyblossom in a lover's embrace and dipped her, kissing her deeply. She took care with her lips, giving the young woman's mouth the delicate attention it had not found in many years. Through her glove, she felt the singer's heart flutter in her chest.

There was a hunger in the woman when Amestoy lifted her back to her feet. "You savage," said Honeyblossom, still brimming with some bizarre disdain even in her lust. "No dog has ever been as lucky as you, to have me."

The singer pushed her fingers down to her clit, parting the robe again. Then she took a step back toward the bed. "Well," said Amestoy looking the painted woman up and down. "I'm not gonna lick you like a puppy. But if you want me to take you, I can take you like you've never been before."

"I want you to try," the singer challenged. The gleam in her eye was clear.

A moment later, Amestoy grabbed for her, wresting the singer off her feet with servo-powered strength as she reached for the bed. "Agh!" the woman shrieked, kicking as her paint smeared gold and pink on the captain's armor.

"Okay," said the captain, hefting her like a small parcel. "Easy now. Over here. Right here against the mirror."

Leaning forward, Amestoy dropped Honeyblossom

back to her feet, pinning her against the suite's mirror with mechanical strength. From this angle, she could stare at the woman's searching eyes as she stood behind her.

"Brute," said Honeyblossom, heart pounding with anticipation. "Brute, I would never—"

"Spit on it," said Amestoy, holding out two fingers of her grey, composite-armored glove. The singer paused a moment, surprised, then spat on the motorized fingers in obedience.

Slowly, Amestoy moved her left hand down, keeping the right vice-gripped on the back of Honeyblossom's neck to hold her in place. "Little Hannah Dunn," the captain murmured. "Always knew she had to make it big. Always knew she had to be the one on that stage, on that cover. All the boys fawning over her. Worshipping her. Fucking each other for her amusement."

The captain's gloved hand made contact with Honeyblossom's pussy, slowly rubbing back and forth as she kept her pinned. The young singer gasped at the sensation, but stayed quiet.

"But there was another little piece of Hannah Dunn," said Amestoy. "A piece that didn't quite fit. A piece that didn't play well with that midworld top-forty marketing crowd. And that was the girls. Beautiful. Powerful. Coy and gorgeous. There was always a little bit of her that wanted a girl to hold her down and take her for all she's worth."

With that, she pushed a gloved finger into the woman. "Oh," Honeyblossom whispered, overwhelmed with feeling as Amestoy clicked her left hand's servos to 'rumble.'

"You're mine, Honeyblossom," Amestoy whispered in her ear. "And if I want you to come, you'll come for me."

With some angling, Amestoy pushed a second vibrating finger up into her. "Oh," said Honeyblossom, moaning as she pressed her forehead to the mirror in rapture. "Oh, you animal."

"Call me what you want," said Amestoy. "I'm freer than you, coreworlder. And I can have my way with you however I like."

Honeyblosson's pussy squeezed tighter around the captain's gloved fingers. Trembling and moaning, she rode the mechanical hand. After a minute, she came, and then at the peak of her pleasure Amestoy threw her face-down onto the bed. Once again, Amestoy's vibrating fingers were against her, this time pressing hard on her clit and vulva. "I want you to really think about it," said the captain, holding the singer down. "Think about this spacer dog you've let into your world. Owning you. Using you up. Now, I want you to tell me you're mine."

"I'm yours."

"You're my bratty little rich girl."

"I'm your bratty little rich girl."

"You're my lesbian whore."

Honeyblossom choked, hesitating. The weight of the word had burned so heavy in her heart for so many years. "I'm," she said, finding new pleasure in the unthinkable liberating mindfuck of the confession. "I'm your lesbian whore."

"You let these boys eat your pussy, and you lie back and think about girls."

"I think about girls," said the singer, arching her back into the vibrating glove now as she choked back tears of bitter ecstasy. "I do, I think about girls."

"And now you're really here getting fucked by one," said Amestoy, and leaned down to kiss the top of the woman's ear.

That was the touch that set her off in her howling second orgasm. She moaned and cried, sniffling and yelping as she rocked with the buzz of the glove. Then Amestoy released her, and she rolled over in a state of melted, doe-eyed putty.

At that moment Amestoy heard the other two people in the room. "Freeze!" she shouted, drawing her pistol in a flash. She aimed it, only to find herself staring down the sights at terrified young Toshi.

"I, uh, forgot my glasses," said Toshi, taking in the sight of pleasure-felled Honeyblossom and her spacer guard. "I had a key card from Bertie. Please don't shoot me."

Amestoy nodded her head toward the exit, and Toshi scrambled off with his glasses. Mag-holstering her pistol, she watched the sense and anxiety slowly return to Honeyblossom's rattled mind.

"My tour," she said, as if Corrine Amestoy could help. "My new album. The press. I'm supposed to get engaged to Duncan Cole next year. I can't do this. I can't do this. But I have to. I can't be stupid."

"That's between you, God, and Bertie to figure out, baby," said Amestoy, walking over to the bathroom to rinse off her power armored glove. "I've hit my limit on free therapy for jaded and repressed."

8 - YELLOWJACKETS

Miles Meyrich did his best to stay calm in the trunk of the New Canberran SUV. "I'm sure Captain Amestoy's dropping everything to find me," he whispered to himself, hoping some mumbled guess would prompt a response from Mia. "I'm sure she's on her way over here as we speak."

He couldn't believe he'd lost his gun and his handset. *That's a Carlotta-level fuckup,* he thought, then laughed to himself as he remembered his old training partner's litany of mishaps. At least he hadn't been killed by a truck while fucking some New Canberran chick in a portable toilet. That would have been a rough one to explain to his aunt.

His thoughts drifted to the woman in the stall. *Yolanda, if that really is your name.*

He had no regrets about fucking her. It was fun, and a total change of pace from having his way with stuck-up and kinky Carlotta. *If this goon kills me, at least I'll still have his girl's pussy juice on my dick when I die. Maybe that's petty. But, hell, I can use all the silver linings I can get right now.*

The SUV stopped after about forty minutes' drive. In

some ways, Miles expected the desert, and he was surprised when they let him out into a suburban two-door garage.

A leather-jacketed dude with a drugged-out slur stuck a gun in his face. "No screaming," the guy said, colorful tattoos across his face and neck. Even in his threats, he had a pain and somehow warm candor to him. "Otherwise I shoot your hands off. That's the rules."

"Screaming, no hands, got it," said Miles. "I like the no-screaming rule, actually, because it goes pretty well with my please-don't-torture-me rule."

The gun-toting, face-tatted guy laughed at the chatty nerves of the kid from the trunk. "To be honest, dog," he said to Miles, "I'm surprised you didn't just use the trunk release and bail."

"What?" said Miles, doing a double-take as he felt around the inside of the trunk lid again. He would have been pretty damn stupid to miss that one. "There's no release. I swear there isn't. I checked like ten times. You're fucking with me."

"Yeah I am," the dude laughed. "Go on, get inside so we can figure out what to do with your dumb ass."

* * *

The interior of the suburban trap house was a mess of ratty couches, card tables, pool tables, fridges, and crates. It was like all the dregs of two dive bars and a warehouse thrown together.

"Sit down," said the forty-year old leader, who had a thick black beard and a scar down one side of his ugly face. In comparison to the guy with the gun, the leader had an angry, unstable twitch to his eyes.

Obligingly, Miles sat on the nearest couch he could find. Then the bearded guy shoved Yolanda up the stairs as she passed. "Get in the bedroom, bitch," he snapped at her. "I'll deal with you later."

"Fuck you, François," said Yolanda, storming off.

The bearded man, presumably François, looked to the gun-toting dude with the face tats and beanie. "Rémy," said François, "keep your piece on this fucker at all times. Shoot him if he squeals. I'll be back."

With that, François went back down to the garage. Rémy sat on the other side of the coffee table, facing Miles as he reclined on another well-worn couch. A plume of dust rose up as he sat, and Miles winced as he coughed with his finger on the trigger.

"Hey, not to critique your marksmanship or anything," said Miles, "but do you mind keeping your finger a little off the trigger if you're gonna be pointing it straight at me?"

"I'm good," said Rémy, and adjusted nothing. "Don't trip."

Miles nodded. There was no clock or holo-screen in this living room, and he could already tell that the minutes spent here would be agonizingly slow. Then he started to think through what little training he'd had at Elektra on the subject of being held prisoner. Building a rapport, he remembered, was the most important step.

"You guys don't really seem like a François and Rémy," he said, nodding toward the man who had gone downstairs.

"They're codenames," said Rémy. "All of us use 'em. Well, some of us. Who's to say which ones, though."

"Uh, well, I would guess that Rémy and François are codenames, and Yolanda is not," said Miles.

Rémy stared at him, but said nothing. Then he perked up again. "Hey, dumbass," he said with endearment, "why'd you have to go and fuck Yolanda anyway? What's your angle?"

"Yeah, that's actually the crazy thing about you kidnapping me," said Miles. "In fact I have no angle, and I have no idea who you are, and I've basically done nothing to deliberately slight or endanger you in any way."

"But you were strapped," said Rémy, "and you fucked Yolanda." He repeated the charge with what almost started to sound like a hint of jealously.

"Yeah," said Miles, "and believe me, if I had known who she was, or who she was to François, I would have stayed the hell away. In fact, I'm a little frustrated with her right now, to be honest. I would just as happily walk away and never see any of you again."

"But you've seen our hideout," said Rémy.

"Uhh," said Miles. "Yeah, because you brought me here. In fact, I didn't even know this was your hideout until you just said it right now. I kind of figured this could be any old place. So, really, maybe you should stop telling me things about your organization that could possibly be incriminating in the first place."

"You's hoping that we let you go, huh?" Rémy laughed.

"Uh, yes," said Miles. "I would say that's a pretty natural thing for a person to hope."

"Okay, sure," said Rémy. "What's your name again?"

Miles struggled to remember the absurd alias that Mia had given him. "Tolstoy," he said. "I do electronics stuff, on vehicle stereos."

"Tolstoy," Rémy laughed. "That's a stupid-ass name."

"Coming from a Rémy and François, I would think you'd have more tolerance for—"

"Code. Names," said Rémy, briefly setting his pistol down to spell out his point with his hands. "They are codenames. We've been through this, Tolstoy. Damn.

Anyway you said you do stereos? Do you know how to bass boost a system?"

"Like, EQ?"

"No, bass boost!" said Rémy. "Damn, I think we deafened your ass when we knocked you outta that bathroom. That was some crazy shit. Definitely put a little newkie heat on us, though. I bet you François's changing out the plates right now."

"I don't need to know that," said Miles. "Don't tell me any of that." Then a loud crash rang out upstairs, and he turned his head quickly to the stairwell at the sound of it.

As he did so, the M5 chip caught Rémy's eye. "What the fuck is that?" the face-tatted man with the pistol said, getting up to cross the room toward Miles. "You a fuckin' cyborg?"

"No, no, no," said Mia, speaking for the first time in almost an hour. "Keep him away. We're still dialing in your location."

Miles considered jumping Rémy for his pistol. Then François returned. "Oi!" the bearded man shouted, shooing Rémy back. "What's the matter with this cunt? Got a robot hickey, eh?"

Miles winced as François tugged on the chip. "Please!" he said, stuttering as he built a lie in real-time. "I have chronic endocrinitosis. That's a gastric stabilizer. All that's gonna happen if you turn it off is I'll have a seizure and shit myself."

François scowled, then made another move to try and rip it free. "Boss!" said Rémy, interrupting him. "Please. I don't need no more shit on these floors, after last time."

The bearded bastard relented, and Miles tensed down. His chip now stung like a motherfucker, but he hadn't noticed any sudden internal shifts. "Shit yourself?" said Mia, not fully hiding her admiration. "Hey, props to you. It worked."

Miles wished to hell that he could ask her where the fuck his rescue team was. Instead, he sighed and settled back into the couch across from Rémy. "Hey whore!" François shouted, climbing the stairs to the third floor. "Do we have any more of that dissolving acid stuff? You know, for bodies."

For the sake of decorum, Miles pretended not to hear that. "Nobody's getting melted today," Mia reassured him through his spine-chip connection. "We've locked you in. Lex and Joe are almost at the house. They're just stuck in a little bit of festival traffic."

Miles coughed to mask his laugh at the absurdity of the statement. "It's that dust," said Rémy, pointing to the particles in the air. "It gets me, too. François don't believe me, but I got dust allergies. Same as my mom."

"Ah," said Miles, nodding politely with Rémy's gun trained on his gut. *This rescue team can't get here fast enough.*

* * *

Captain Amestoy rode in the armored car with Honeyblossom from the hotel to the festival's main stage. "Two hours to show," a radio crackled.

"Thank you, two," a makeup tech sitting across from the spacesuited captain responded.

The light was still strong at six o'clock that evening, in the scorching heat of a New Canberran summer. Amestoy felt the rumble of the engine as the car advanced through the underground traffic tunnels connecting the hotel to the performance complex. "Great way to avoid fans," she murmured. "Terrible place to get hit with an ambush."

Honeyblossom hadn't looked at her since that afternoon. Whatever tumult of self-reflection and practical concern had overwhelmed the singer, it was too much to allow her to continue even the slightest small talk with her unexpected paramour.

Amestoy was fine with the silence. It was better than the constant line of insults which had wandered out of Honeyblossom's mouth before she'd fucked her lights out.

"Captain," her handset crackled, faint in the tunnel since she'd turned off her connection to local relays. It was better to keep *Aurora's* communications off of the newkie-run lines.

"Yes, Engineer," said Amestoy, responding to April Zamora.

"I don't think Lex and Joe know where they're going," said April. The captain could hear a lingering concern in the woman's voice. "Requesting permission to take the monorail east and help put eyes on target. I don't want to leave Operator Meyrich hanging out to dry any longer than we have to."

"Granted, but eyes only," said the captain. "Don't turn it hot before our pros show up."

Orson had already canvassed the backstage, running a KALI-assisted scan before Honeyblossom's armored car showed up. When Amestoy exited the vehicle, she did a double-take at his new banana-patterned shirt.

"Best order you ever gave me," said Orson, laughing as he pointed to it. "My skin can breathe. It stays cool. I'm quicker on the draw. Maybe I'll start wearing this for every—"

"*No,*" said the captain, then winked before stepping to the side to let the singer pass.

"Not the friendliest VIP, huh?" Orson murmured to the captain, once Honeyblossom had made her way over to her dressing room.

"It's complicated," said Amestoy.

* * *

The sea of festivalgoers waiting in the field beyond the stage was so dense and alive that it felt more like a natural, surging force than group of people. "These fucking sightlines," Amestoy muttered, looking at the two-dozen structures that would give a sniper's scope a dream view of the concert stage. "I should've told Ji-Yoon we can't really do shit once she goes on."

"I just had to trust the feds and the newkies to keep those towers clean," said Orson. Then he stepped out into the evening light, pointing to a twinkling cruiser overhead. "Ropeburn's giving us some overwatch from *Aurora,*" he added, "but unless we want him dropping insertion rounds, his hands are pretty tied."

"Bullshit that they gave her such a high-strip cruising window," said the captain, increasingly irritated with the security situation. "*Aurora's* doing active angel work, and they've got her up in the fucking mesosphere."

Orson shrugged. "Saves fuel," he said. "And at least we got that one maniac taken care of."

"Only that creeper doesn't bribe his way out and come back to finish the job," Amestoy grumbled, setting her suit's helmet down on a nearby shelf to recalibrate it. "I swear, if they weren't so stupid I'd say the newkies were setting us up to fail."

Honeyblossom pushed past them again, heading out toward the rear loading dock of the performance complex. "I need a smoke," she said, trying to get away from a big-bellied guy in a suit and glasses.

"Smoke? Honey, your voice..." the man whined, pushing after her.

"Fuck you, Bertie," said Honeyblossom. "Wait inside or

I'm quitting the Magna tour."

Sufficiently scared, Bertie paused, sighing as he watched Amestoy follow the singer out onto the loading dock. "Oh, what, your little guard dog gets to come?" he called out to Honeyblossom. "Your little spacer, but not your best bud Bertie?"

"You're not armored and packing," Honeyblossom called back.

* * *

Captain Amestoy stepped out into the violet-tinged evening light, leaning against a grip truck full of lights and scaffolding. Its suspension creaked as it took the weight of her helmetless power armor.

Honeyblossom turned away from her, trying and trying to get a cigarette lit. After ten tries, the lighter was spent, and the singer was almost crying as she held the bent smoke on her lips.

"I got it," said Amestoy, her first words to the woman in hours. Then she flipped her armor's right wrist panel open and pressed the tip of the cigarette against the battery element.

It came alight, and Honeyblossom took a shaking puff. After ten more seconds of silence, she held it ever so slightly out towards Amestoy.

The captain took a drag, tasting the ash and the flavor of the pop star's lipstick. Then she stared at the long, empty road and abandoned industrial buildings ahead. Outside of the glitzy ten square blocks of the festival grounds, New Canberra was in a state of perpetual semi-decay.

"We shouldn't be out here," said Amestoy. "This sector's not covered."

The singer took the cigarette back. A minute passed,

then two, with the light fading and the cigarette burning to nothing all the while. Then the captain noticed a faint glint behind one of the third-floor industrial windows.

"Do you think," Honeyblossom started, with words she had been working on for quite some time. "Do you think you'd ever—"

Then Amestoy saw the blinking red light of a micromissile launcher armed to fire. "Get down!" she shouted, tackling the singer mid-sentence as they dove behind the bulk of the parked commercial truck.

The missile fired, breaking through the glass of a third-floor window across the street as its operator pulled the trigger. Soaring straight for the loading dock, it fell short, scattering across the pavement with an explosionless clang.

Honeyblossom raised her head to look, but Amestoy pushed her down. Then the missile exploded with a small grenade's worth of force. The captain held the singer tightly, cradling her and shielding her from the blast, as it blackened the front of the parked grip truck.

Amestoy's ears rang from the shot, but she knew she hadn't been hit. Checking Honeyblossom for shrapnel, she raised the woman to her feet, then shoved her inside as another missile's arm-light flashed in the abandoned building across the road. "Stay with Orson!" she shouted, slamming the heavy door of the backstage complex shut.

She still didn't have her helmet. "Motherfucker, motherfucker, motherfucker," Amestoy grunted, using each repetition to count the seconds until the micromissile's delayed fuse would ignite. The second missile went long, bouncing off the stage door, then tumbled into the grip truck's open back. *I hope you've got insurance,* Amestoy thought as the explosion shredded hundreds of thousands of credits worth of gear.

The captain didn't wait for a third light to blink. Drawing

her heavy slugdriver pistol, she aimed high and took her best guess on the shooter's distance. Without her helmet overlays, she'd need to eyeball the bullet drop. *Blam!* She fired one shoulder-kicking round, stabilized by her stance and her suit's armor servos. *Blam! Blam!*

After three rounds, the red light shone again. Then a micromissile fired upward, clumsily ascending toward the cloudless sky before exploding like an underwhelming firework. Then the missile launcher itself tumbled from the third-floor window, followed by the bloodied shape of an adult man.

Amestoy grabbed for her wrist radio as she watched the man tumble into an overflowing dumpster. "Shots fired, shots fired, target down behind the music complex. Moving to apprehend."

"I'm here with the VIP," Orson's agitated voice came back. "Should I move to romeo?"

"Fuck, uh, negative," said Amestoy. "Stay with her. Where's everyone else?"

"Miles is kidnapped," said Orson. "April, Lex, and Joe are headed to extract him."

"God damn them," said Amestoy, but did not transmit it over comms. Running, she crossed the cracked asphalt and reached the dumpster where the wounded missileer had fallen. "Okay, dynamo," she said, grabbing for him as she stood on her toes to look up over the side. Instead, her glove gripped only disintegrating trash bags.

Then a burst of small-caliber bullets hit the dumpster. Two glanced off the armor of her back, causing a chest-shaking thud as the metal deflected them. That was way too close of a call without a helmet. "Fucker!" she shouted, continuing her string of curses as she swung her pistol around to face the shooter.

The gunman was the wounded missileer, aiming a disposable plastic pistol from the driver's seat of a six-wheeled white, unmarked van. He was a young guy, maybe twenty-eight, with a few days of brown stubble on his gaunt face. He wore glasses, and had long hair more fitting for a surfer than a would-be assassin.

The shooter ducked, throwing his pistol out the window, as Amestoy fired. Her slugdriver round passed over his head, making spiderlike cracks on his van's windshield as it punched through the glass. Then, with his head still down, the shooter floored the pedal and peeled off down the empty industrial road.

Where the fuck is festival security? Where the fuck are the newkies? How the fuck did this guy smuggle military hardware fifty yards away from the VIP? Lacking answers to any of those questions, Amestoy settled for sprinting on servo-assisted legs after the van.

The physical properties of her own joints, unfortunately, were the bottleneck in setting her top speed. Around twenty-two miles per hour, her legs started to strain, whipped back and forth with each cycle of the motorized suit's running gait. "Republic command, anyone," she shouted on an open emergency line. "I need aerial support on a white Stuart Crosshauler. Ji-Yoon? Ji-Yoon can you hear me? Come on!"

The heat sensors in her suit's joints chimed, and the captain gave up chasing the van on foot. Panting, she stood still, her legs tingling from the nervous strain as she watched the six-wheeled van accelerate away.

Then a bolt of white light cracked through the New Canberran sky. It was an orbital insertion round, delivered with a touch from *Aurora's* belly gun to the middle of the abandoned street ahead. It missed the van, perhaps on purpose, instead catching it in a shockwave which sent the vehicle spinning and careening on its side.

The shockwave, and the rumble, tore through the city block like a sudden earthquake. Car alarms went off in the distance, and windows shattered as a hot, dirty wind washed over Captain Amestoy's face. Then, as it dissipated, the roar of the blast and the hum of the van's engine turned to silence.

The van's wheels squeaked as they spun in the air, hanging from its overturned chassis. The doors were shut, and there was no sign of life from the brown-haired shooter within. Despite that, Amestoy wasn't about to underestimate him again.

"Not the lightest touch, Cap," tactical officer Ropeburn's voice crackled through on her wrist computer. "Sorry about that. I made a split-second call."

"You did good," said Amestoy. Then a chorus of sirens filled the air, drowning out the sizzle of the crater-shaped blast site. Like ants reacting to a colony intruder, ten angry newkies poured out of blue-and-orange sedans and trucks to contain the scene.

"Captain," said KALI, speaking to Amestoy over her wrist comms. "I'm seeing unusual activity inside that van on my spectrographs. Stay alert."

"What kind of activity?" asked Amestoy, and a moment later a furious newkie officer gripped her by the arm.

"What the fuck have you done?" he asked, making a move to pull her away from the crime scene. His ceramic armor was nothing compared to her powered suit, and after a moment of embarrassment he gave up trying to manhandle the woman.

While he glared at her, four more newkies jogged toward the van. "I'd be careful!" Amestoy called out to them, but they paid no attention. "Just saying, guys."

"Captain, cover," said KALI. "Cover now."

Just then, the back doors of the overturned van blew open. A teeth-shaking, high-pitched whine rang out, and Amestoy could tell at once from the sound what was waiting inside. A second later, twelve backpack-sized suicide drones burst out into the evening air.

The drones swarmed like enormous yellowjackets. "Down!" Amestoy screamed at the four advancing newkies, but they were too far ahead to take any cover. She fired her slugdriver, kneeling behind the hood of a patrol sedan, as six of the twelve drones exploded into shreds on contact.

The ceramic armor did little to stop the drones from tearing the newkies apart. Their ripped and shredded bodies fell, lifeless, as the other six drones acquired Amestoy and the officers around her as their next best targets.

During this, the bloodied shooter pushed out the van's front windshield. "Hey!" the captain shouted, but had no time to fire on him as he sprinted across a nearby boulevard. It was all she could do to shoot at the swarm of screaming suicide drones.

A combined hail of fire from the captain and the newkies put down the drones before they could reach the patrol cars. "Officers down!" the one by Amestoy screamed, holding his handset in a panicked grip. "We need all units, all shuttles here at grid eighteen-nine. Suspect still at large."

All over the intersection, other newkie patrolmen were making similar pleas for backup on their own radios and handsets. From the chorus of dispatch responses, it sounded like the whole of the New Canberran Independent Authority was inbound.

"I'm pursuing," said Amestoy, shaking the officer out of his shocked daze. "Back me up or not, but don't let your guys shoot me."

"Okay," he mumbled, nodding. A second later, she was sprinting off after the shooter again.

9 - RAID

Miles and Rémy were on their third game of chess at the east city safehouse. "Move the knight up," Mia Rain told him through his implant, appraising the board through his M5 chip's sensors as he took a swig of expired beer. It had been better to accept it than refuse it, Miles had thought.

The captive operator made his move. "No, the other way," Mia grumbled. He deliberately ignored her as he let go of the piece. A second later, Rémy killed the knight with an incoming bishop.

"You're really bad a chess, dog," said Rémy, on his second beer.

"I told you that," said Miles. "I barely know how to play."

Upstairs, François berated Yolanda again. "Jean-Jacques!" Rémy called out to a guy down in the garage. "They almost here?"

"They're here," said a scary-sounding guy down below.

They? Miles watched Rémy stand up, losing all interest in the game as he glanced outside. François was descending the creaky stairs, and Miles took one last moment to try and get a little kindness from his captors. "Rémy," he said, "listen, I'm just a car speaker guy. I'm not even from the planet. If I go, I'll buy the next ticket off this rock, you'll never hear from—"

Rémy shushed him, eyeing approaching François. "Later," he whispered. "I got you."

Miles was shocked. He wasn't sure what to make of this, but the merciful look in face-tatted Rémy's eyes certainly seemed sincere. Regardless, he hoped his rescuers would come before he ever had to see the gangster's kindness tested.

A group of unfamiliar men climbed the exterior stairs to the safehouse's second-floor entrance. Miles watched their blurry shapes through the curtains, then jumped as they slammed the wood door with four loud knocks.

"Coming!" shouted bearded François, who may or may not have mumbled 'self-righteous cunts' as he opened the door with a grin.

Four suited, long-haired syndicate types entered, carrying mag-driven automatic weapons. *That's some serious heat,* Miles thought as he watched them size up the room.

"Who the fuck's that?" said the syndicate boss, pointing straight at Miles. "He wasn't on the dossier."

"Just some middie acting childish that we gotta scare straight," said Rémy. "Don't trip."

"He won't be around much longer," said François, making a slicing motion against his own neck. That seemed to satisfy the syndicate guys enough.

"Who are they?" asked Mia, as if Miles had the faintest idea. "Can you point the side of your neck straight at him? That's the spot where the sensor's best. I wanna scan his face and see if he's a bounty."

Miles turned his neck toward the stairs, to allow Mia a better view. As he did so, he saw Yolanda staring down from the top of the steps. They made eye contact, and she stayed stone-faced before heading back into the bedroom.

A newkie shuttle buzzed the top of the house, flying low overhead as it raced toward the festival square. François looked jumpy, but the syndicate boss calmed him down. "Scanner's lit up with some shooter at the Honeyblossom concert," the long-haired boss explained. "All the newkies are distracted. Little bit of an unexpected blessing, so let's not waste it. You got the credit bars?"

"What the fuck kinda question is that?" said François, taking a coarser rhetorical approach than the smooth-slicked syndicate crew. "Yeah I got 'em. You got the Jupiter?"

Miles rolled his eyes at the big reveal. *Drug deal. Wonderful. I'm sure these guys dish out all the overpriced glitter those midworld kids were rolling on.*

A midworld kid himself, Miles found himself surprised to be thinking of them as a whole with such disdain. Maybe it was April Zamora's local sensibilities rubbing off on him. Then his thoughts turned to the purple-haired engineer, and he realized that she was the person he most wanted to stay alive for. It wasn't out of any love or affection, but from the guilt he knew she'd carry if he died. They were partners on this mission, after all, and it must be a terrible to kiss somebody for the first time right before they die.

While he'd been lost in thought, the syndicate guys had brought an armored case into the trap house living room. It looked heavy, maybe fifty pounds, and they opened its lid to reveal back after bag of glittering, pure Red Jupiter. It was a decent fortune's worth of product.

It made some sense to Miles that the syndicate guys had brought out the Jupiter first. After all, they were certainly well armed enough to defend it if François tried to rip them off. The bearded gangster knelt, scanning the bags with an electromagnetic sensor through the plastic. Then he called out to the man downstairs. "J.J.," he said. "Bring our friends their credits."

"Big buy for a small operation," said one of the rifle-toting syndicate analysts. "I was surprised when your guy said you wanted twenty-five kilos."

"What, you think we live in this shithole?" said François. "Let me tell you something, man, I've got condos offworld. I've got a lakehouse on Kaiten."

"I was only saying," said the analyst, "that we're impressed with the growth you've achieved as an independent outfit."

François nodded, aware that he'd been needlessly combative with the man. From downstairs, Jean-Jacques appeared with a case of encrypted credit bars. "Five million even," he said, presenting the case to the syndicate boss. "Go ahead and scan it."

While the syndicate guys authenticated the digital credits in the case, Rémy and his pistol slipped across the room to Miles. "When I go out front, you haul ass out the kitchen door," the gangster whispered to his young captive. "J.J.'ll be here, but he ain't got no gun. Don't stop running till you're free."

Miles nodded, afraid to say anything back. He wished Mia would chime in with an ETA on his rescue. Without any intel, it was hard to know whether staying or running was the riskier move. Then, as if on cue, he heard the voice in his spine again. "Miles," said Mia Rain, sounding genuinely alarmed. "Miles, get down. Now. Get down now."

There was an odd 'thump' on the wood front door. "Rémy," said François, snapping his fingers. "Go check that out."

Rémy stood, walking toward the front door. Listening hard, Miles could hear a creak, and at the last moment he saw the tiniest shadow of a black-clad form through the window.

Face-tatted Rémy opened the safehouse door. Then his head exploded.

"Lex, no!" Miles shouted without thinking, watching the gangster's skull and brains paint the couch where he'd just sat.

It wasn't Lex at the door. The figure was a tall man dressed in black, with tactical armor and black clothes conspicuously devoid of any markings. Only his brown eyes and pale coreworlder skin could be seen beneath his dark balaclava. He held a smoking shotgun in his hands as Rémy's headless body fell.

The syndicate guys panicked, swinging around to fire at the door. Before they could, two more figures in identical black riot armor burst through the windows. With cold, efficient fire, they let their submachines guns rip through the midsections of the syndicate men and François.

It was only Miles' seated slouch that kept him alive. He dropped, cowering, as the men with the cash and the Jupiter fell in bloody piles. Some of them were half ripped apart by the hollow-point rounds, and huge holes tore through the opposite wall wherever the bullets had landed. *That's major fucking firepower.*

"Upstairs," one of them said to another, pointing to Yolanda's bedroom. Miles could only hope the woman had an escape route.

There was no escape path for him. Pushing his hands feebly in the air, Miles yelped as the first black-clad shooter aimed his shotgun straight at the privateer's forehead.

"Please!" Miles shouted, his mind screaming with noise. "Please don't shoot! I'm a privateer!"

The shotgun-wielding man hesitated. Then Mia's voice came through. "Miles, I'm gonna dose you with something right now. You gotta use it. Okay? Two seconds."

Miles wasn't sure what the words meant, or that he would survive the next two seconds with his brain intact. Then he noticed something gleaming at the shotgun-holder's waist.

It was a federal police badge.

The badge was hanging partially out of a pocket underneath the man's black vest. It clearly wasn't supposed to be visible now. The man looked down, fully aware of what Miles had seen, and tucked the badge back into his inside pocket. Then his finger tightened on the shotgun trigger.

At that moment the stims from the M5 chip hit Miles' brain. He was confused for a moment, watching the federal cop freeze as if paralyzed. Then he realized it was time that was distorting itself for him. In surreal slow motion, Miles threw himself to the left. It felt like it took a good ten seconds for the action to complete.

The shotgun glowed with fire as buckshot danced out of it, burning like embers from a sparkler. All of it sunk deep into the foam of the couch. Lurching forward, Miles slid past the guy, calculating his actions with care as time progressed in a dreamy meander. *This is going to give me a hell of a hangover.*

Miles' fingers settled on the pistol which had fallen from headless Rémy's warm hands. *Alas, poor Rémy,* Miles thought, and in that thought he realized that his fear and panic were gone. Whatever Mia had pumped him with, it had to be more than just an ultra-strength time-dilator.

Killing the cop felt almost like chess. Miles took his time, considering the fear in the man's eyes as they turned ever so slowly to track him. The shotgun itself was swinging around like a huge construction crane. Before the barrel could reach him, Miles lay the pistol's tip comfortably against the neck of the cop's balaclava. He pulled the trigger, and like a rising tide the pistol grip pushed him backward.

It also placed a bullet deep inside the cop's cloth-covered neck. Going limp, the man began to fall, and Miles turned his attention to the back kitchen door that the late Rémy had mentioned.

SMG fire slammed the oven and fridge, chasing Miles as he ran out the back door. Sprinting for his life, the young operator leapt the hurdle of the backyard fence, continuing forward through a small section of suburban desert scrub.

His sense of time was returning to a frantic, heart-pounding normal. "Run!" Mia shouted. For her, his escape from the shotgun cop had only been a few seconds prior. "Straight! Now hard right! Down the drainage trench!"

Miles pulled his arms in, rolling sideways down a concrete drainage half-pipe that ran from the neighborhood into a paved-over riverbed. The riverbed was waterless, and under a nearby traffic bridge three *Aurora* crew were waiting.

April lifted him to his feet while Lex and Joe trained their rifles on the sandy bank above. "Miles!" April shouted, dusting him off with a voice of incredible relief. "What the fuck happened in there?"

"Deal go bad?" Joe asked, watching the street. "So predictable."

"No," said Miles. In the sudden withdrawal from the time dilation, he was struggling to remember even the faintest details of the last sixty seconds. "No, I don't think so. But I think we should run."

"Double-parked the whip," said Lex, pointing to the navy-blue shuttle *Sanpi* sitting in the riverbed thirty feet away. "Fuck those newkies."

"They got their hands full anyway," said April, clambering inside the shuttle with the rest of the team. "C'mon, next stop is backing up Captain."

* * *

Captain Amestoy followed KALI's guidance, running northeast across the boulevard as automated construction trucks blared past. Crossing a pedestrian bridge, she descended two sets of graffiti-soaked stairs, climbing through a hole in a barbed wire fence to arrive at an abandoned mall.

"I'm watching the exits," said Ropeburn over comms. "He's somewhere in that complex. It's too thick to penetrate on thermal, so I can't do a lot unless you want me to bunker-bust the whole thing."

"Negative on the showstopper," said Amestoy. She reloaded her slugdriver, taking a breath as she sized up the dark and dilapidated mall. "Do you have decent visual on the hot zone?"

"Affirmative," said Ropeburn, "except when these bloody party-yacht cruisers float right over it. I'd love to drop down a few bands into the troposphere."

"Just do it," said Amestoy. "Aisha? Ana Sofia? You copy?"

"Copy that," said Ana Sofia. "Dropping straight down through ten layers of traffic. Let the angry comms begin."

"I'll try to use a diplomatic touch with these civilian captains," XO Anwar added.

Captain Amestoy turned around, hoping to see at least a few bold newkies crossing the road toward her. Not a single one of them had left the site of the van crash. Aside from the creep in the abandoned mall, she was totally alone.

The sunset had turned blood orange, almost black. "Captain," said KALI. "While Tactician Ropeburn can cover the surface exits, there are a number of subterranean corridors through which the target may be able to escape the complex. I suggest you apprehend him before he discovers them."

"Ah fuck," said Amestoy. "I was afraid of that. How long till I get my enforcers?"

"Fifteen minutes at current heading and speed," said KALI. "Operator Meyrich and Engineer Zamora are also onboard the shuttle."

The captain took a breath. Ahead, the crumbling corridors of the mall loomed like a spiraling cavern. "XO Anwar, remind those newkies not to blast me if they ever decide to breach the mall. KALI, tell the *Sanpi* team to form up on my signal when they land. I don't have my helmet, so my comms are open-air through my suit. Take me off this channel unless it's an emergency, okay? Otherwise he'll hear me coming a mile away through all your chatter."

"Good luck, captain," said Orson. "The VIP says 'good luck,' too."

"That's very sweet of her," said Amestoy, and advanced toward the decrepit mall with her pistol drawn.

10 - CAPRICORN

Miles felt like there were ten-pound rocks wedged above each of his eyes. He lay on the floor of the shuttle *Sanpi,* watching the atmospheric pressure lights on its grey ceiling blink. In atmosphere, the engine roared, and city lights flashed color through the windows as Joe Avar piloted the craft through thick skylane traffic. After dark, the teal sky of New Canberra became a splash of advertisements, illegal fireworks, and occasional bursts of refinery flame.

Lex Rockbridge loaded and checked the magazines of a rack of light-fire rifles. "Disruptors, smoke, incendiary," he muttered to himself. "Shock rounds. Hammer rounds."

April Zamora knelt over Miles, listening to the hurried instructions of Mia Rain over her communications earpiece. "Okay, take the C3 vial," said Mia, talking April through the insides of the shuttle's first aid pack. "Now put it into the injector unit. Prime the needle. Carefully. Carefully! It's not a spaceship thruster, Engineer."

"I'm doing my best," April hissed. Miles laughed in pain as he watched her roll her eyes at the doctor's voice. It was nice to have someone else stuck with Mia Rain inside their head for a change.

A new wave of withdrawal effects came over him, tingling and cold. "I can't feel my chest," he said, throat cracking. His skin as if it had been soaked in ice water from his nipples down.

"That's his nervous system shutting down," said Mia. "The C3 should balance him out, but you've got to get it straight into his carotid artery."

"Where the fuck is that?" said April.

"His neck," said Mia. "Turn on the bio-light on the front of the injector. You should see it in blue. Shine it over him. You see anything?"

"I think so," said April. "Miles does this feel right, right here?"

She touched her finger to his neck, against what she hoped was the artery. "Uh, I have no idea," said Miles. "Just go for it, or soon I'm not gonna be feeling anything at all."

"Okay, here goes," said April, straddling him and pressing the unit against his skin. The needle jabbed him, and Miles winced as it pumped the purple C3 fluid into his circulatory system.

Miles felt the feeling return. Then he began to shake in a twitching, uncontrollable hot flush. "Doc, he's vibrating," said April. "Oh god. Did I kill him?"

"Nope, you hit the money," said Mia Rain, looking over Miles' surging vitals from *Aurora's* med bay. "His muscles are overreacting to the stim. Maybe, uh, apply some pressure. That should help it pass."

"Pressure where?" asked April, looking over the kid in the jeans and Sashimi Beats tee.

"Everywhere, ideally," said Mia. "I usually use a restraint press for this."

"Okay," said April. Hesitant, she lay his shaking arms out. Then she pressed her body against his own like two layered starfish. Her tattoo sleeves pressed against his fair, muscular biceps and forearms. Her jeans lay on his, feeling his hip and leg muscles shake.

She turned her head to the side, speaking in his ear as her cheek touched his half-day of stubble. It was a shocking feeling to her, the scrape of his coarse sandpaper skin, after years with a woman. "Is this better?" she asked him, trying to apply even pressure to his limbs and chest.

"Yeah," said Miles. "Yeah, yeah, that's way better."

"Doc, what the fuck are you telling these kids?" said Lex, looking up from a filled light-fire magazine. "I never saw that in no CPR guide."

"I don't question your shooting, Enforcer," Mia jabbed back over the shuttle speakers. "Don't question my medical methods."

"Shuttle *Sanpi,* you're flying like a fucking twat," some luxury cruiser pilot yelled over the front comms. Joe kept his cool, turning the radio volume down as he powered forward.

"You're not gonna yell at him?" Ana Sofia said from *Aurora's* bridge, adding her voice to the chorus on the line. "Okay, Joe, I'll yell at him." Then she switched to the skylane band. "Hey, *pendejo,* check his clearance and move to the right. It's republic law."

April's handset chimed for the third time since she'd climbed aboard *Sanpi.* "Uh, you can get that," said Miles, who'd stopped shaking half a minute prior. "I'm fine now."

"Right," said April, returning to her knees and helping him up. She grabbed her handset, dismissing the notifications, and sighed before stuffing it back in her pocket.

"Scammer?" said Miles, watching her grumble.

"Huh?" said April. "No, just Nicki."

"Your girlfriend," said Miles. It was something he'd wanted to know since he'd first met the two of them in the mess hall.

April didn't know how to answer that. "I don't think so," she said, shaking her head and pushing her purple hair back. "She's just… somebody I've felt responsible for, for a long time."

"Oh," said Miles. He didn't know what to make of that, but it sounded heavy. "I see."

"Okay, babies, lock and load," said Lex, tossing April a light-fire rifle. "I know Maeslon's run you through the gauntlet at least once, but lemme give you a thirty second refresher on how not to blow yourself up."

He offered Miles the second light-fire rifle, but Miles declined. "I'm good," said the operator, grabbing a replacement Featherhand pistol from the locker. "I'll stay mobile."

"I'm losing the captain's signal," said Joe, refreshing the cockpit scanner. "Stay prepped and ready for a quick drop, boys and girls. Who knows what kinda shit she's got herself into."

* * *

Captain Amestoy turned off as many lights on her power armor as she could. Her steps were heavy, crunching as stepped over broken bottles and rebar. Still, she wanted to do as much as she could to avoid walking into a trap.

The main floor of the mall was a bizarre, trompe-l'œil mess of styles. Its main drag was themed like a rustic coastal villa, and a dried-out canal cut through the middle where water had once flowed. Beyond it, faint echoes of broken holograms danced above a sim-plex and a shuttered arcade.

There were a million places this guy could hide. Without her helmet, she had no thermal scanner, and any thousands of knocked-over shelves or statues could have served as workable cover. *Maybe baiting him out is the only move.*

"Hey weirdo!" she said, taking a stab at the guy's profile based on what little she'd seen of him. "I bet you thought you were so much smarter than all those dumb fucks at school. But where are they now? At home, watching TV and fucking their wives. Meanwhile you're holed up in some filthy mall, about to get your shit pushed in by newkie lead."

"You did this!" a man's voice from the second floor shouted, scared and deranged. The captain spun around to train her slugdriver on the sound, but saw only darkness above. She held her fire.

"I did what, blew your wheels up four seconds into your getaway?" she laughed. "Yeah I did. Nice going, dude. Did you forget starcruisers exist?" She paused, waiting for an answer, then added a lie. "Your shitty drones didn't even kill a single one of those newkies."

"Leave me alone," the man repeated. "I don't want any feds in here. Not after what you did."

"What I did?" said Amestoy. She took a moment to check her wrist computer, hiding behind a broken carousel. No comms had come in since she'd entered the mall. "Listen, man. There's only one way this ends. Now, I can guarantee you'd rather get picked up by me and handed straight to republic intelligence, instead of getting fucked by some newkies on the way to the city impound. So, I'm coming up there, okay? And the longer it takes me to find you, the worse this gets."

"I'm sorry," said the man above, and there was the sound of a long zipper opening in the dark. "I tried to warn you."

A new, higher, softer sound of buzzing drones filled the echoey atrium of the abandoned mall. In the blackness, Amestoy heard an insectoid swarm of metal blades drawing nearer. With a snap, she switched on her shoulder lights, aiming her pistol to see three dozen sawdrones bearing down.

The drones were small, softball-sized gyroscopes fitted with engines and circular, toothed razor blades. Each one had its own pathing intelligence, just complex enough to keep it from crashing into its sisters as it searched a space for human blood. Amestoy had seen them before, and their handiwork on the gashed-up faces of outworld civilians. She knew she did not have the time, ammunition, or aim to kill them all before they reached her.

Dropping to the ground of the canal floor, she lay flat, covering her exposed head with a nearby manhole cover. It was all she had time to do before the drones closed in. They rattled and shrieked as the chopped at her armor, cutting small chunks of paint off the steel in lieu of their preferred flesh. Around her hands, they gashed at the kevlar-composite, cutting so deeply that the blades touched the skin below the glove. She brought her elbows tighter together, praying that none of the robots would find a path to her face.

Then she heard boots in the atrium, through the drone-whine. "Oh fuck," Miles Meyrich's voice murmured, seeing the captain face-down and swarmed by piranha-like sawdrones. Then, one saw him, and then the whole pack was swarming toward the t-shirted operator.

"Fuck, Lex, disruption!" he shouted. "Lex, disruption!"

Gold-toothed Lex Rockbridge grabbed for an ion-pulse disruption emitter grenade on his tactical belt. "It's gonna fry our gear, kid—"

"Do it!" said Miles, firing at the drones as he prepared

to be cut-into. Just as they reached him, Lex's ion blast went off, and the drones fell to the ground as a dozen nearby holograms went out.

"Fucking hell," said Amestoy, feeling at the brand new chunks in her armor through sliced gloves. "There go my comms."

"All our comms," said Joe, "and optics."

A light rattle of footsteps on the upper level made Miles turn, shooting off a round into the dark. The steps continued, and the drone-wielding assassin settling into some new hiding place in the black of the mall.

Amestoy sized up her team. Miles was in plainclothes, carrying a Lightbringer pistol. Lex and Joe were in half-fried tactical gear, both holding loaded light-fire rifles. April, without any combat experience, held her own rifle awkwardly at her side.

"I'll take that," said Amestoy, grabbing April's light-fire rifle for herself. It was more of a liability than a boon in the engineer's novice hands. "Zamora, I'm gonna need your mind on this one."

The captain put her armored arm around April's shoulder, walking her through a gameplan. Miles nudged Lex's plated pauldron, scanning the upper floor for hostile threats all the while. "Hey," he said, "you got a twenty-slip shock mag for me?"

Lex fished in his bag, drawing a single blue-tipped bullet meant for a Featherhand pistol. "Just one round," he said, as Miles pushed it into the chamber of his weapon. "Why shock?"

"Little more kick through circuit boards," said Miles. "Who knows how many more robots this fucker has up his sleeve."

He turned to see April ascending a broken escalator in a

calm, almost sleepwalking gait. "Psst!" said Miles, rushing forward to pull her into cover. "Get down!"

Amestoy held him back. "Let her walk," said the captain, watching as April stepped up onto the atrium floor. "Let her walk."

"Hello, friend," said April, her voice taking on a goddess-like quality in her reader's trance-state. She spoke to the blackness of the upper level, and to the would-be assassin hiding within. "I can feel your fear. The pain in you. You know how all this ends. What's that you're hiding behind? It's a colorful thing. No, don't close your eyes. I can still see its memory in your mind. It's… a *Nebula Force* arcade machine."

As April said it, reaching into the man's frayed mind, Lex shined an underbarrel flashlight on the front of the second-floor arcade. Behind a purple-painted video came machine, a faint shadow shifted.

Lex and Amestoy opened fire, shredding the machine in a blast of sparks. "Agh!" April screamed, reeling from the secondhand pain a bullet hit the missileer in his side. She broke the mental connection, collapsing on the ground at the top of the escalator as the twice-wounded man scrambled out the arcade's back door.

The captain vaulted up the escalator steps, passing April as she gave the suspect chase. Miles followed, but stopped to kneel at the engineer's side as she sobbed and gasped. "I felt it," she said, clutching her uninjured side. "She shot me. I felt it."

"You're okay," said Miles, as Lex and Joe brushed past to follow the captain. He cradled her in as warm of an embrace as he could give. "I've got you, you're safe. You're not going anywhere. I'll stay with you here."

April shook her head negative. "Go help the captain," she whispered, clutching his head as she looked into his eyes. "He's headed to the M-Line. She'll need you there. I'll be right behind you."

Then she shoved him back to his feet. Miles helped her up, dusting her shoulder off where tiny chunks of broken glass had stuck to it. Then he took his pistol in two hands and chased after the two enforcers.

"Fuck, I lost him!" shouted Amestoy, stopping at a place where his trail of blood went cold. Ahead, four paths extended in different directions out of the covered mall. She tried her dead comms again in growling frustration. "Ropeburn, do you have eyes on the suspect?"

Of course, the lifeless receiver gave no answer. "M-Line," said Miles, pointing to an arrow at the second passage's entrance. "This way."

Captain Amestoy trusted his appraisal without question. "On me," she said, and he followed her up the darkened hall with Lex and Joe close behind.

* * *

The sound of rumbling bass rose up as Miles reached the abandoned monorail terminal. It stood eight stories above the street, serviced by high-speed elevators that had never been completed or installed. Past the end of the platform, a single three-foot-wide concrete rail extended west toward the festival district.

Amestoy was the first one out onto the platform floor. She charged in her black-and-red powered boots, pounding pavement until she reached the unfinished monorail track.

The shaggy-haired suspect was running at a sprint down the monorail track, a bulky grey hoodie over his thin body. On both sides, the eight-story drop became a twenty-story drop as the elevated street gave way to a sunken festival pit below.

There were thousands upon thousands of partiers in the

distant pit. Rave music washed across them, along with colored sights and streamers in the neon-soaked night. Support columns for the monorail track rose up from the pit, continuing until the pillars and the track reached an incomplete end. After the last one, the raw edge of the half-built monorail track gave way to empty air.

"Got you, fucker," said Amestoy, smacking the side of her slugdriver to turn on its underbarrel laser sight. Behind her, Lex threw his flashlight on the suspect. Then the man turned around to reveal a twelve grey-wired packages strapped to his chest.

"Charges!" Miles shouted, instinctually ducking behind a monorail platform pillar. It was a move he had practiced many a time, when paint-spraying robots had attacked him during training in the form of facsimile suicide-bombers.

"He's too far to hit us with that payload," said Amestoy, loud enough for the suspect to hear. She was unflinching as the crazed man held out a blinking dead man's switch. With a press of his thumb, he armed it, setting the vest to detonate as soon as his hand went limp or pulled away.

"Yeah," the man called back, "but I can blow these pillars and squish a couple hundred Jupehead party kids under falling concrete."

He was probably right. *Fuck, Ropeburn, I hope you're putting in a call to clear out the festival pit,* thought Amestoy.

"Even if *Aurora* gets word to the newkies," whispered Lex, elbowing Miles on the monorail platform, "it'd take 'em half an hour to clear the pit. Not to mention the panic in the crowd."

Miles nodded. He knew it, and he could tell the captain did, too. "Okay, man," said Amestoy, keeping her laser sight trained. "You've got my attention. What's the next move? You didn't come here to kill college kids, or you would have opened with it."

"Honeyblossom," said the man, arms outstretched as he swayed on the thin concrete track. Miles worried that he might accidentally blow the charges just from losing his balance.

"What about her?" said Amestoy. "You already blew her to pieces."

"Liar!" the man shouted. "I saw you save her, you fucking fed."

"I'm not a fed," said Amestoy, which seemed to change the man's whole visage from anger to despondent shock. "I'm Corrine. What's your name?"

"They didn't tell you?" he asked her, incredulous and aggravated. "I'm Capricorn."

"Capricorn," said Amestoy. "Okay. I'm a Scorpio. Listen, why would a smart guy like you want to waste your time killing Honeyblossom, of all people? Trust me, I've met her. She's boring."

Miles aimed his Featherhand pistol at the man fifty yards down the track. He hoped the glare from Lex's flashlight would be enough to keep the man from seeing him as he adjusted. "I could drop him," said Miles, murmuring to Joe Avar. "I could hit his hand."

Joe shook his head. "Anything you do, he might let go and blow the thing, even if you drop him with a skullshot. Muscles get weird when a man dies."

"How many have you dropped?" asked Miles, sizing up the clean-cut enforcer with the toothpick in his mouth. He hadn't taken Joe for a hardened killer.

"Enough," said Joe.

Up ahead, Capricorn and Amestoy were continuing their high-stakes chat. "Believe me," the man with the explosive vest pleaded, looking for some twisted understanding. "It wasn't my idea. She's a sweet girl. I never wanted to do it. But it made me. This is all part of the plan, you know? Alpha Sixty. The end of the world. The realignment of the meta-human paradigm."

"*It* made you?" said Amestoy. "What made you?"

Capricorn looked at the captain as if it were obvious. The he let out a shaky, fearful breath. "Idolex," he said. "Idolex told me. It sent me the guns. The drones. The ticket."

As the man rambled, the warm night wind picked up, and a new thought came to Miles' head. "I've got a shock round," he whispered to Joe. "If I hit him center mass, it'll stick. The current'll keep his thumb squeezed on the dead man's switch."

"So what, he falls and hits the deck like a bomb?" said Joe. "That'd be worse."

"You're right," said Miles. He opened up the side of the pistol, examining a dial that controlled the intensity of the shock-round burst. "Unless it blows in mid-air. Look. He's past the last pillar. If he falls backward, and he blows halfway down, he'll be far enough away that it might not hit the tracks."

"That's a big fuckin' gamble," said Joe, spitting his toothpick onto the concrete of the platform. "Maybe we better let Captain talk him down."

Miles watched the eyes of the desperate man flick. With each new piece of information Amestoy shared, he grew closer and closer to the brink of a mental breaking point. *There's only one way he's ending this thing, and it's not clean.*

The young operator did as much mental math as he could in his head. Then he remembered the M5 chip still planted on his neck. "Hey, Mia, you there?" he asked.

A moment passed, and he felt a chill cut through the skin

around the chip. It was too sharp and timed to be a coincidence. "You're there," he said, "but you can't transmit voice 'cause of the disruption blast. Is that right? Do it again if that's right."

The sudden ice-cold feeling came again. "Okay," said Miles. "Do the newkies have a handle on this? Flash that cold-thing again if you want us to just keep stalling."

Nothing came. April, behind him, watched with curiosity as he continued his one-sided conversation. "Okay, then we're fucked," said Miles, and another chill confirmed it. "In that case I need you to have KALI do some math for me."

Miles turned to the side, pointing the center of his chip's optics sensor toward Capricorn. "See that guy?" he asked. "I'm gonna shoot him center-mass with a shock round. I want you to run some physics sims and tell me how many seconds to set the stun for. 'Cause as soon as the stun ends, his thumb's gonna slip off that switch and he's gonna blow. That's gotta be right halfway between the track and the crowd. Got it? Now I'm gonna go in half-second increments, and you buzz me when I hit the right number. One-half. One. One-and-a-half. Two."

Nothing came through. April scowled as she watched Miles continue to count. "Four. Four-and-a-half. Five."

His neck again turned cold like an ice cube had pressed it. "Five," said Miles. "Really? Five? That feels like way too much. Are you sure?"

The cold came again, and he shivered as he felt it spreading into his temple and throat like a brain freeze. "Whatever drug you're signaling with, I hope it's not toxic," said Miles. Then he turned the dial on the pistol almost to the max. "Okay, five seconds for the gold. You and me are gonna be in some deep shit if this doesn't stick, KALI."

No further signals came through the M5 chip. Squaring

up his stance, Miles aimed at Capricorn, sensing the wind as he adjusted his lead and the bullet drop. "Don't fuck this one up."

A new song faded up at the DJ pit below, with Honeyblossom's remixed lyrics sunk into the synthy morass of the beat. "Every day you smile, and our love gets stronger," her pithy vocals swooned.

The sound of it pressed new agitation into Capricorn's skull. "Look at me," said Amestoy, extending a hand to bring him keep him tied to reality. "I'm gonna come out there, okay? Then we can disarm this thing and start the rest of our lives."

She took a step out onto the concrete track. Foot by foot, she advanced, her ripped glove outstretched as she kept the slugdriver at her side. In the distance, fireworks popped above downtown, causing Capricorn to spin with fear as he turned to see them. Then he relaxed. "I'm here," said Amestoy, and in the firework light the man calmed as he saw her face.

Then, from the distance, the teal-and-orange lights of a newkie patrol shuttle flashed. "Drop the weapon!" they shouted through their speakers as they neared. Miles couldn't tell who they were talking to, until their glaring spotlight lit up the man on the ledge.

Capricorn almost fell as he whipped around to see them. "Go away!" he shouted, almost childlike as he yelled at the shuttle's roaring engines overhead. "This is between me and Corrine!"

"Drop the weapon or we will fire," the shuttle loudspeaker repeated. *Fucking idiots,* Miles thought, watching Capricorn as the man looked down at his dead man's switch.

The captain waved for the shuttle to back up, but it was too late. With an apologetic look, the man with the explosive pack looked to Amestoy and began to slowly loose his grip.

Miles took the shot. With a light 'crack,' his single shock-round left the Featherhand's barrel, arcing like a curveball with the wind and gravity as it crossed the distance to Capricorn. Before the shaggy-haired man could react, the round buried itself in his heart, causing him to writhe as it blasted him with electrical impulse.

One second. Two. Three. Miles watched the seizing body stumble back, not quite falling from the monorail track. Then it tumbled off the edge.

Four. Five. A blast like a thick orange firework shook the sky above the DJ pit. Four stories below, three thousand partiers looked up in unison, then cheered at the vanishing fireball above. The music went on, and no panic set in as the smoke from the compact charges dissipated. Miles grimaced to think of the man's dispersed body parts landing among the ecstatic, Juped-out crowd.

"Hope he was totally vaporized," Joe laughed, echoing Miles' thought.

Amestoy turned to face Miles, confused for a moment as the adrenaline of the moment coursed through her. Then she understood. With a nod, she reassured him, then turned to point an angry finger at the shuttle above. "You stupid fucking bastard," she shouted at the newkie pilot. "You better thank your fucking saints that this kid saved you from killing two-hundred people."

The shuttle loudspeaker said nothing, perhaps sufficiently shamed by Amestoy's scolding. It backed up and turned off its spotlight as the captain peered over the edge of the unfinished track. From the look of the revelrous crowd below, you never would have known how close they'd just come to disaster.

Miles turned back to April Zamora, sighing from the stress of the moment. "Holy fuck," he said, catching her brown eyes as more fireworks danced across her face. "Holy fuck."

"Yeah, holy fuck." said April. He wasn't sure what he'd expected her to say. "Not bad for a guy pumped with drugs and stuffed in a trunk. When we get back, you'll have to tell me how you got yourself grabbed, by the way."

"Maybe," he said, embarrassed and exhausted at the thought of sharing that story. "Or, maybe not. I think my nerves are plenty spent for one day."

11 - PAYOUT

Amestoy scanned her hand into *Sanpi's* biometric ignition as soon as she got onboard. "I'll take us up," she told Joe, who ceded the pilot's seat as she kicked the shuttle into gear. As soon as the comms module loaded, she got on the line with Orson and XO Anwar. "Aisha," she said. "Disruption fried our comms. Everyone's safe. Ship status?"

"Nominal," said Anwar. "That was an impressive shot from Operator Meyrich."

"It was bloody insane!" Miles could hear Ropeburn shouting in the background. He looked forward to watching a replay of the moment from the eyes of *Aurora's* thermal ground cameras.

"Copy," Amestoy said to Anwar. "Orson, we're dusting off from hot zone to romeo with you. How's our VIP?"

"Pissed," said Orson. "She's forty minutes late to go on stage. I wouldn't let her leave the dressing room while you were out of contact. Should she go on now?"

"That's a call for Ji-Yoon," said Amestoy. "This whole

situation's way hotter than what we prepped for. See if you can get her on the line."

"I'm right here, Corrine," said the republic intelligence officer's measured voice. Even through the call, something in her Ji-Yoon's snakelike tone made Miles shiver. "You did well out there. Let's get our starlet up on stage, and get you and your team some rest. The threat is neutralized."

How the fuck can you be sure? Miles thought, but kept the question to himself. He sat next to April on the shuttle bench, listening to Amestoy as she coordinated endlessly across four different comms channels. The captain's responsibilities during a planetside snafu like this were not something to be envied.

Soon, *Sanpi* landed in a commercial loading zone one block over from the Hotel Grandeaux. "Hey hotshot," said Orson, bringing Miles into a surprising hug as the shuttle door opened.

"Orson!" said Miles, finally tensing down as he saw the enormous man smile. "Wow, great shirt."

"Oh yeah, I guess you haven't seen this yet," said Orson, tapping the banana print. "Some days you save the day, some days all you get is an overpriced shirt. I guess we can't all be superstars like you."

"Aw, come on—"

"I'm serious!" said Orson. "Ropeburn won't shut up about the shot you landed. Neither will that crazy pilot of mine. They've been talking my ear off on comms since you bagged him."

"KALI did the math," said Miles, shrugging modestly. "I'm just glad nobody else got blown up with that fuckin' whacko."

"So am I," said a voice that made Miles' legs go weak. He turned, almost giddy with fatigued disbelief, to see a fifty-year-old man with a trimmed goatee walking toward him. The man was suited like Ji-Yoon, but wore a republic colonel's pin on his black lapel. Miles knew him in an instant as Lord Isaac Stahl.

"Holy shit," said Miles, shaking a little. "I mean, I'm so sorry. I mean, Lord Stahl, it's an honor." He had to force himself not to salute out of army-school habit. The man was shorter in real life, but possessed the exact same spark of charisma that he did in newsreel footage and on propaganda posters. "I had action figures of you, sir. Well, I imagine all of us did."

Lex shrugged. "I don't know who this guy is," he said, flashing Stahl a polite, gold-toothed smile. "You the big papa fed on duty?"

"You did a great thing, son," said Stahl, staring Miles straight in the eyes with an unexpected intensity. "The republic owes you a debt."

"Just take these fucking newkies out of business," said Amestoy. "Best thing you could do for this place is set up a real state government. None of this outworld territory crap."

Lord Stahl turned to her, tapping the pin of the republic flag that sat just above his colonel's rank. "We're working on it, Captain," he said with a small smile. "Outworld four-two is a part of my administrative district, after all."

April suppressed a yawn of fatigue as she listened to Amestoy and Stahl discuss the operation. "Get these heroes home," said Stahl, and it was absurd for Miles to hear his childhood idol describe him as such. "They've earned a break, Corrine. You did your part."

"Colonel," said Orson, asking what Miles had been wondering. "Respectfully, how are we supposed to walk away from our VIP now? Who knows how many vans full of suicide drones that freak coulda parked around town."

"We're handling it," said Lord Stahl with finality. "Go home, bounty hunter. It's over."

"Don't need to tell me twice," said Lex, tossing his light rifle into *Sanpi's* weapons rack. Joe spooled up the shuttle, and after a shake between Amestoy and Stahl the team set off for *Aurora*.

* * *

The finer points of the past day's events were too much for Miles to even begin to process. He spent the ride back to *Aurora* in silence, feeling like he should by all counts be exhausted beyond belief. Instead, he felt strangely electric, and it was with joy that he realized he was leaving a combat mission without any serious injury—even if the time dilation had done a number on his nervous system.

"God could I go for a steak," said April, who had been writing paragraphs to someone on her handset since they'd touched off from New Canberra. "Garlic mashed potatoes. Asparagus. Maybe a cold Firestalk IPA."

"Oh, yeah, talk dirty," said Miles, fake-moaning at the imagined meal. "Throw some grilled prawns in there, too."

"Damn, you been here two weeks and you're already that pressed for shore leave?" said Lex.

"Shore leave?" said Miles. "Nah, I'd do dinner in the engine room at this point. I don't care. I'm just tryna fuckin' eat."

"Facts," said Joe. "I would take one day's shore leave, though. Maybe get my dick wet over on Makwak Station."

"Bleugh," said April, miming gagging. "I'm fine with not hearing any dick-related details, thank you."

"Don't knock what you ain't tried," said Joe, before getting up to go stand behind the captain at the front. "Hey, Cap. What do you think about some shore leave for us heroes?"

While he made his case to Amestoy, Miles turned to April in a hushed murmur. "Was he coming on to you?" he asked, somewhat stupidly. If there was any component of possessiveness in his question, he didn't want to admit it.

"No, it's just a bit they all have, on *Aurora,*" said April, rolling her eyes. "I'm surprised your roommate didn't tell you already. She always gives me shit for it."

"Ana Sofia? Gives you shit? For what?"

April scowled at Miles. *Was he fucking with her?* Then a brief glimpse into his emotions revealed his sincerity. "For never having been with a guy," said April.

"That's dumb," said Miles. "It's 'cause you're with Nicki Stafford. I mean, I know you said you're not, but—"

"I guess," said April. "It's not, like, a thing. I mean, I've kissed guys."

"You kissed me."

"Oh yeah. And plus, I had boyfriends back home as a kid—"

"Mele?"

"Yeah for a day, in third grade," April laughed. "Mele's been head-over-heels for one of our other friends as long as I can remember."

"I'm sorry we didn't get to meet your old buddies," said Miles, remembering the big game they'd talked about an inner-city reunion. "That would have been fun."

"Yeah, well," said April. "Maybe some other time. But it's for the best. I've got a price I've gotta pay when we get back to *Aurora,* and I may as well just get it out of the way."

* * *

When *Sanpi* docked, Miles learned that dinner prep still had an hour to go. He scarfed down two protein bars, followed by a bag of flourless chips and a glass of juice. Then he headed to the armory to stow his pistol and boots.

Sergeant Maeslon was servicing a chaingun when he walked in. The red-haired woman was short and strong, maybe thirty-four years old. She wore a perpetual viking scowl, and carried deep skepticism in all matters Miles.

Her strong jaw tensed. She wiped her hands, pushing the gun aside on the workbench. She wore cargo shorts, and an olive short-sleeve tee over her workout bra. "Meyrich," she said in her stiff, frigid accent. "Stupid move. Computer cannot calculate body physics so accurately as you think. You could have blown the train bridge."

"I know," said Miles. "But it woulda blown anyway if I'd just stood by. Sergeant."

She walked up very close to him and threw her oil-stained mechanic's rag to the side. "You are a cocky midworlder," she said, leaving a black mark on his tee where her finger touched his sternum.

"Hey! This is Ropeburn's shirt," said Miles, stepping back and rubbing at the stain. "Now I gotta wash it before it sets."

"First chore you've ever done in your life," said Maeslon. "And I bet you won't even do it. You'll go ask KALI for help like the baby you are."

The sergeant was right about that one. Rolling his eyes at her, Miles pulled the Sashimi Beats shirt over his head. Then he walked down the hall until he found KALI's hovering, silver robotic body. "Hey," he said, showing the shirt to her. "Do you think the machine'll get this stain out? What setting should I use?"

"Hot, with the 'spot clean' setting," said the synthetic

intelligence. Miles thanked her, then went to the aft to toss the shirt into *Aurora's* onboard laundry processor.

As Miles turned to go grab a new shirt from his bunk, he felt Mia Rain's familiar voice in his spine again. "Operator," she said, in a tone full of pent-up mischief. "Do you think you won our little game?"

Miles scoffed at her question. "Do I?" he asked. "I almost got myself melted in acid, just to satisfy your little creep mind. I think that's more than enough."

"I agree," said Mia, to his surprise. "And I have your reward right here, so report to the med bay. That's an order."

* * *

Miles Meyrich entered the med bay shirtless in his belt and jeans. The light was brighter than the rest of the ship, and kept cool even when the rest of the hall lamps were turned a nighttime yellow. The windows to the hall were switched opaque, and the sliding door shut behind him as he came into the room.

Just ahead, Mia Rain stood in her red-and-white glossy medical jumpsuit. Her blonde bob was brushed and set, and her youthful nineteen-year-old face scrunched into a smile as she saw lean young operator enter. "Welcome to my secret laboratory," she said. "I see you got the dress code memo."

Miles glanced around. He didn't see any credits, or whatever other gag gift she may have prepared for him. "Is my reward getting this chip out?" he asked. "Because that would be a pretty raw deal."

"Hardly," said Mia. With a digital tablet cradled in one arm, she pressed her hand to a biometric lock on the back wall. "Please, this way."

A door which Miles had assumed to be a closet slid open.

Inside, there was another white room, as small as a bunk but devoid of furniture. At the far end, a window looked out *Aurora's* starboard side, into the void of space. In the center, a white motorized examination table lay flat.

April Zamora was completely naked and restrained on the medical table. She lay on her back, with her arms and legs strapped down on white-cushioned table arms. Each table arm was articulated, adjusted so that each limb could be individually pivoted in snow-angel-type motion.

She was also blindfolded, gagged, and fully earplugged. There was no reaction from her as Mia opened the door to the back office. She lay in total audiovisual deprivation, breathing rhythmically as her ribcage moved up and down.

Her head was toward the window, with her toes and bottoms of her feet closest to Miles. Her vulva was shaved, and Miles blinked in surprise as he saw her thin lips and dark-pink clit. He had never seen a girl this undressed in such detail, or in such full light.

April's auburn nipples were small and hard, rising and falling atop petite breasts that lay half-flat on her lean chest. With this vantage, Miles could see just how much of her was covered in tattoos.

"What the fuck?" Miles laugh-mumbled in sudden reaction, taking the whole sight in with a single blink as the door opened. "That's Engineer Zamora."

Mia tapped a button to shut the sliding door, sealing herself and Miles in the back room with the splayed and clamped-down purple-haired young woman. "Your reward," she said. "For the next thirty-eight minutes, till dinner time."

Miles exhaled, running a hand down the back of his close-cropped head. He could already feel his dick starting to rise from the unexpected sight of the naked woman. It was surreal to see her like this, completely restricted and exposed. It still felt like mere moments ago that he'd stared into her eyes at the festival bar.

"I guess you want me to fuck her," said Miles, forever the one to ask the obvious questions.

Mia didn't answer, but her face could not contain her little smile. "This is your operation, Meyrich," she winked.

"And you're gonna stand right there?"

"I'll position myself as needed to observe," said Mia Rain. "This is vital to my research, after all."

"I thought this was supposed to be *my* reward," said Miles. Then he did another double-take as he looked at April Zamora's wet pussy ready for the taking. "What the hell did you do to her, doc? Did you drug her?"

"No," said Mia. "Although I did tell her that she can't do any reading while she's here. Look, you can see it on her vitals. This spot'll pop up in her brain if she tries any empathic outreach."

"Weird," said Miles, getting a smell of Mia Rain's expensive perfume as he stood near her. The scent, like her silky bob, seemed more fitting for a society woman than a nineteen-year-old prodigy on a starcruiser. "What if I fucked you?"

Mia Rain blinked at the words, looking up. He watched her free hand linger near the crotch of her jumpsuit. "That would be," she said, "outside the rules of engagement, Operator."

Miles nodded. "Fair enough," he said, cracking a jokey smile. The surge of nerves from the night's combat had left him feeling worn-out and smooth. "You're too young for me, anyway, doc."

With that, he took a slow walk around the side of the table, taking a good look at April's tattoos and figure. She was like a fine piece of art here for his inspection. Mia Rain stood by as the broker. "Can I take her blindfold off?" he asked. "Her earplugs?"

"If you wish," said Mia, scribbling a note on her digital tablet when he asked it.

Miles nodded. Now he felt like a bull in some alien breeding program. His dick was pressing hard at his jeans, creating a small open tent of denim and cotton at his beltline. He removed his belt, unbuttoning the top of his jean buttons. He loved the feeling of prim, button-nosed Mia Rain watching it all with hungry eyes.

He moved a hand almost to April's head, ready to remove her blindfold. Then he paused. It still didn't look like she even knew if anyone was in the room. Then, moving his hand down, he placed it ever so gently on the place where hard-breathing ribcage ended and her abs began.

She gasped at this touch, seizing up for a moment as she reacted to the feeling. He hadn't expected such a strong reaction. Delicately, he pressed his palm against her body. He slid his hand up, listening to the sound of skin on skin as he approached her left breast. The nipple turned even stiffer as his forefinger touched it, circling it with measured interest.

Then he walked slowly backward, letting his hand run along her as one might run their hand along a couch's back while passing it. He felt her little waist, her belly button piercing, and the bone of her hip as he passed the ridge. As he went on, he let two fingers slip toward her vulva, brushing the clit and lips. Then he reached her legs, squeezing her calves, before at last interlocking his fingers with her toes.

He felt her squeeze his hand back with her foot. It was a small, charming feeling. He considered putting his cock against her foot, letting her feel what she had never felt as he rubbed it across her naked legs and shoved it inside her. Instead, he walked back to her blindfolded head and knelt near her right side.

Gingerly, he removed one of her earplugs. Then he slowly lifted the blindfold up to her forehead. She blinked, squinting under the bright medical light. Then she turned, looked at Miles, and smiled at him with the breathless surprise of seeing a long-lost friend. "Miles," she said, lips dry from her nerves. "I didn't think it was going to be you."

Miles wasn't sure what that meant. "Well, I definitely didn't think it was going to be *you*," he chuckled. Then, almost without thinking, he laid a hand on her chest and pressed her right breast down as he touched the nipple.

She gasped at the feeling, staring straight at him. "I tried to warn you about Mia," she said with a smile.

"What do you mean?" said Miles. "Her game?"

"She put in my M5 two months ago, after I got caught in thruster blowback," said April. "She talked me into the same game as you. But I chickened out halfway. I lost. So, she told me I had to come get fucked by someone of her choosing, whenever the right moment arrived. I mean, I could have protested. But fair's fair."

Miles nodded as he listened. "Well," he said, "we don't have to——"

"No," said April, cutting him off. Then she looked a little bashful. "No, I mean. You should. But, only if you want to. Otherwise I understand. I know I'm nervous, and if you don't think I'm attractive, well…"

Miles quieted her rambling by pulling the blindfold back over her eyes. "Shhh," he commanded, and slid her earplug back into her ear. She was breathing even quicker now, moving her hips ever so slightly as her ass pressed against the examination table. Once again, she was sightless and deaf as he looked over the curves of her body.

Strutting around to her feet, Miles spread the articulated leg-restraints slightly apart, causing the lips of her pussy to slightly spread as it tensed and swelled. Leaning in, he watched it, smelling her sweet scent and touching her inner lips with his fingertips. With his thumb, he raised the hood of her clit, pressing his own mouth against it as she shuddered. That was his second good kiss with April Zamora today.

Then he stood and let his jeans and underwear fall to his ankles. As he did so, Mia Rain stepped forward from her place at the wall, getting on two knees as she took a measurement of his rock-hard cock with a small device. He half imagined grabbing her head and shoving his dick in her mouth as she knelt next to it. *Perhaps some other time, with more invitation.*

Then he realized that she planned on staying right there, kneeling a just a foot away from the action. With April's legs spread and Mia's blonde bob beside his hip, Miles took hold of April's waist and pulled her forward.

The whole apparatus moved toward him on a lubricated arm, leaving April's ass half hanging off the central table. A little further, and her whole ass was free, firm and ready for him to grab from below as he penetrated her.

Angling himself, Miles pulled the table a few inches upward, to his dick height. Then he tilted his dick slightly down to find her vagina. She moaned as he pushed her lips aside, listening to the sticky sound of her arousal as he nestled his cock's head against her. Her ass was cold, and he felt his hands warming it as he pulled the cheeks slightly apart. Then, with an overwhelmingly pleasurable thrust, he slid inside of her.

April Zamora was the tightest of the three women he'd ever fucked. Carlotta had been thrilling in the victory of conquest, and even Yolanda had been amazing in her enthusiasm and lust. April, however, was the warmest and most perfectly shaped thing he'd ever had the pleasure of sticking his cock into.

He slid into her again and again, feeling his hips touch the insides of her thighs as he filled her up. He was half thrusting, half sliding the movable table back and forth to use her like a handheld fuck toy. Mia Rain stood now, leaning over the side of the table to get a closer top-down view of the fuck. "Acceptable?" she asked, watching Miles' thick cock press in.

"Yeah," said Miles, breathless as he used the engineer's tight pussy harder and harder. "Yeah, if you had a dick, doc, I'd say you've gotta try it."

"I can get a decent understanding from your brain activity," said Mia, flipping through her tablet to review his M5 readings.

"What about her?" said Miles, pausing a moment to let his hard cock throb inside of April. She was twitching some, but couldn't express much else through the tight restraints.

"Her?" said Mia, flipping to another page containing Zamora's vital. "Oh. Oh yes. She's feeling better than you are."

Miles almost took this as a challenge. He leaned forward a bit, humping into April solely for his own hedonistic satisfaction. He sucked her nipples, biting a bit at one, and squeezed the sides of her ribs as he pulled her body toward his.

Then his eyes fell again on her face. It was a beautiful face, kind and warm and not so pretty as to be impossible or pretentious. Her neck was tensed, and her cheeks were reddened as she threw her head back with a grunt. In that moment, he wanted nothing more than take her face and ravage it with everything he had.

A low, incredible rumbling rose up around the base of his cock and balls. It was an oval-shaped vibrating silicone puck, controlled by Mia Rain's tablet as it rose up from the end of the table to massage April's pussy and Miles' taint. Try as he might, he couldn't stop the combined force of the pleasure from making him come.

"Oh, I'd fuck her twice a day!" Miles moaned as his cum shot into her, hot and yearning. The buzz of the silicone puck was overwhelming, and he shuddered as he pulled his dick out, dripping cum and pussy juice on the backroom floor. "I swear to god, I wanted to screw her cute little brains out since she smiled at me in the mess hall."

He didn't even know if that was true, but it sounded good. He was still hard, and still burning for her as he saw the buzzing puck shift against her vulva. "You're getting her off?" he asked Mia, watching the doctor adjust a slider on the tablet. The young doctor's other hand was pressed covertly against her own vulva through her jumpsuit. "So much for clinical distance, huh, doc?"

Then his attention turned again to April's wonderful face. Panting, he stumbled around to her head, stepping out of his pants the rest of the way. It was then he saw that her earplug had at some point fallen back out. "Hey," he said, lifting her blindfold up. She was ready for his blue eyes this time. "Hey, you want to try a cock in your mouth?"

Through throat-clenching waves of building, vibrating pleasure, April gave her friend the tiniest nod. At this, he took a fistful of the purple hair on the back of her head, pushing forward to slide his hard and dripping cock into her mouth.

April moaned as she tasted her juices and his cum. Her mouth was warm, tongue was coarser than her pussy as it lapped at the side of his dick. Her teeth touched lightly at the base as sucked hard, still restrained. Then the silicone buzz reached a fever pitch, and she came with an overwhelming burst as she let the cum and fluid and cock all spill across her face.

By the time she finished, Miles was a tiny bit soft, still standing at her face with the head of his cock comfortably inside her cheek. She looked up at him with bright eyes, red-faced and drooling, as he stroked her hair.

Miles took a step back. Restrained and light-headed, April looked his naked body up and down, swallowing in contentment. He could tell that he was like nothing she'd ever taken in before. "I hope," she said, swallowing again to clear the spit from her mouth as she laughed. "I hope that was okay, for you."

He laughed in surprise as Mia Rain took another set of notes. "Um," yeah, he said, touching her warm breast and side again. "Yeah, that was perfect."

"Ten minutes to dinner," Erik Hansen announced over the intercom. "Everybody wash your dirty mitts. Especially if you went planetside."

Mia swung the pivotable table forward, so that April went from lying back to nearly standing in her restraints. April tensed her pussy again, and cum dripped from it as Mia manually opened each clasp. The engineer stepped out, still shaky from her pounding orgasm, and stumbled as Miles rushed to catch her by the waist.

He held her for a second, both of them dripping and naked on the white plastic backroom floor. Then he got her to her feet and let her go. "Doc, we better get cleaned up," Miles said to the blonde nineteen-year-old who had been quietly touching herself through her clothes. "Unless we want to show up to the mess hall like this."

April laughed in an ugly, charming burst of surprise as she imagined the scene. "That would be, uh, a shitshow," she said, and brushed her hair back as she leaned against the wall. In this room, at least, she had no clothes to change into.

Mia Rain procured a towel for Miles. "You can do the honors if you want," he said, raising up his arms to show off his athlete's form as he presented his semi-soft cock to the doctor. In lieu of toweling him dry, she simply tossed it onto the table arm beside him.

Miles wiped the spit, cum, and pussy juice off his dick and balls. "Don't forget," he said to Mia, pointing a finger at his chip. "I still need this thing outta my neck."

"I can do it right now," said Mia. "Give me three minutes. It's easy. Then, please, shower."

12 - GANGBUSTERS

The chip removal turned out to be 'easy' for exactly one insidious reason—Mia Rain had no planes to remove its cybernetic baseplate. "It's not worth it," she explained to annoyed Miles, "given your line of work. It would be too hard on your body to keep taking the plate on and off every time you need stims. If it really bothers you, I can fabricate a cover panel color-matched to your skin."

"No, it's fine," said Miles, rolling his eyes at the fact that she'd conned him into a cybernetic implant. "I'll leave it silver. Take a page from Engineer Miyachi's handbook."

Newly de-chipped but still with a baseplate in his neck, Miles grabbed a full-sized towel and walked down to the communal second-floor barracks showers. To his mild surprise, Engineer Zamora was the only other person in the room.

He took the showerhead opposite her, a few feet away in the humid and steam-filled room. As good as it had been to cover himself in sweat and bodily fluids, it felt equally good to wash it off after a long field day. "How come she took your baseplate out, not mine?" he asked Zamora, assuming some tone of casual conversation.

"Because I'm not supposed to do field work," said April. He couldn't tell where exactly her mind was at now, four minutes after reaching a climax of uninhibited passion. "It's not in my contract. Today was an exception."

She seemed concerned, almost cold. "Hey," he said, nudging her black-inked arm with his elbow. "I'm sorry, if I, uh—"

"What?" she said, turning to him with sudden rapt attention. They stood only one foot apart under the falling water. "No, no, no. Miles. You have nothing to apologize for. You're wonderful. It's just me. I'm messy. Sometimes I don't know… I don't know."

She sighed, bowing her head and resting it against his wet chest as she sighed. The slightest edge of his semi-soft dick brushed against her bare hip as they breathed together. Even after fucking the daylights out of her, Miles couldn't help but feel like this was some new, intimate level.

The doors to the shower room slid open, and he saw Ana Sofia in the hall with her gym bag. She held a folded towel at her side. "Hey, Serrano," said April, smiling at her with ingénue light as she sniffed back her worries.

"Yeah, hey, come on in," said Miles, but Ana Sofia did not enter the room.

"I'll shower later," the pilot said, and Miles watched his roommate continue down the hall.

Miles scowled. "What was that?" he asked, looking at April. "We're not doing anything wrong, right? I mean, Nicki, you said she wasn't your—"

"It's not you," said April. "I just, I don't know. I just need to figure some stuff out."

Miles nodded. "Okay," he said, washing up quickly and

throwing on his casual shipboard uniform. "Well, if you want a friend, here I am. If you want some space, just say the word. There's plenty of space out here."

"Infraction," KALI's voice came through the intercom, reminding Miles that she was omnipresent on the main ship's deck. "*Aurora* charter bylaw sixty-eight. No 'space' puns."

"Ah, fuck," said Miles, slapping his forehead with his palm. "I guess I gotta re-read my handbook. C'mon, Zamora, or we'll miss all the steak and potatoes."

* * *

Despite Miles and April's collective manifesting, the menu for the night turned out to be linguine and spinach. Miles scarfed three helpings down, stopping at Orson's light suggestion before he made himself sick. "Macros," said Orson, sliding him a side-dish bowl. "Eat some chickpeas too. Thirty-nine grams of protein per cup."

"If I do my scan tonight and I'm not at a deficit, you can punch me," said Miles, chowing down on a piece of garlic bread instead. "I ran my ass off all day while you tanned on a hotel roof."

Miles sat at his usual table with Orson, Ana Sofia, Ropeburn, and moody, eyeliner-wearing cyberwarfare specialist Caleb Li. Ana Sofia called it the 'cockpit crew,' since three of the five spent most of their time up in *Aurora's* bridge. Orson had been granted provisional membership, on account of being Ana Sofia's regular squeeze. Miles, perhaps for lack of any other friends, had also been granted a place at the six-seater table through his status as her bunkmate. Many attempts had been made to turn XO Anwar, the most notable bridge regular, into cockpit crew's sixth member. Anwar had declined, ostensibly because of her heightened rank, but Miles felt that Ana Sofia's constant allusions to anal sex had to have played a role.

"Fuck me in the ass," Ana Sofia grumbled, this time as an expression of frustration and not flirting. "I gotta switch the fuel line. I forgot. Evelyn's been waiting."

Ana Sofia ran off toward the engine room to find Evelyn Miyachi—who did not eat, and rarely attended social meals despite Amestoy's encouragement. Through the gap she left, Miles looked up, and at once made eye contact with April Zamora.

April was three tables down, sitting with frizzy-haired Nicki Stafford on her arm. Around them were some lower decks crew whose names he could never remember. When Miles saw her staring, he smiled, but quickly looked down as busied herself with her pasta.

"Captain!" Cook Erik Hansen called out, handing Amestoy a plate as she entered the mess to a round of applause. "What's the big payout for bagging that psycho?"

"Don't start spending yet," said the captain. "It's a total fucking shitshow on this one. There are three parties looking to us for damages, including the newkies—"

"Fucking bullshit!" shouted Ropeburn, who had as usual begun drinking stout once his shift on the belly cannon had finished. A few other crewmen joined in, jeering not at the captain but indignantly on her behalf.

"I know," said Amestoy, putting out her hands to urge calm. After so much time seeing her in her armor, it was a trip for Miles to watch her now in her casual uniform. There was no one in the galaxy who could bend an angry, ragtag crew into an army like she could. "I know, it is bullshit. But it's the cost of playing the game. I think we can shake most of it. Our bounty license does a lot, and so does our legal team. But, Nicki and Grace, it's gonna be a lot of long nights for the three of us this week—and I don't mean in a fun way."

Miles turned his eyes to Grace Burdette at this. She was

sitting with Maeslon and Anwar, making the most of her place at the officers' table, and had reserved a second seat for when Amestoy eventually sat down. It was funny to see her done up so properly again, looking so downright conservative in her fashion, when the memory of her indecent, red-faced self was still so clear in his mind.

"But tonight," said Amestoy, raising an icy glass of the galley's new rice beer. "Tonight, we don't worry about any of that. Tonight, we celebrate our away team. Our shipboard operations team. And the kid who saved two hundred good-for-nothin' midworld lives."

It was sincere, glowing praise from a captain who granted it sparsely. Miles beamed, allowing himself a small pageant-queen wave of appreciation as he took in the chorus of cheers from the assembled crew. Lacking a rice beer of his own, he grabbed Orson's, and raised it in a toast. "To you, Captain," he said, and another slightly louder cheer followed.

Orson let Miles keep the beer. "Alcohol's not in the meal plan, anyway," he said, logging another cup of chickpeas on his handset. "Hey, where'd my pilot go?"

"To change the fuel lines," said Miles, and wondered if he could really be so tuned-out by now to her talk of ass-fucks. "With Evelyn."

The muscular specialist nodded, once again wearing a signature black fitted tee. Then his thoughts returned to the legal quagmire on New Canberra. "Fucking viper," he said, and Miles somehow knew he was talking about the intelligence agent Ji-Yoon. "You'd expect federal police to have our backs, for the shit we do."

Federal police. The term roused something in Miles that he had forgotten. It was frightening, like remembering bad news that one would sooner forget, and he hated the feeling that came up inside his chest as he thought it. Nonetheless, he had to continue searching for the rest of the broken memory. "I thought she was republic intelligence," he mused.

"She is," said Orson, "but in the outworld the intel spooks lead FPB raid divisions. Sketchy shit, I'll tell you that."

Raid divisions. Miles felt a lump in his throat. "Orson," he said, not sure how to explain what was forming in the depths of his stim-scattered consciousness. "Orson, I think the FPB raided the house, before I got extracted."

"And what, they just let you walk?" said Orson. "Hell of a coincidence. Planning those raids takes months. And if you had been in the house, you probably would've been taken into custody just by association."

"Not if I—" Miles began, and cut himself off with a sharp pang of fear. *Not if I killed a cop and escaped.*

Then he remembered who had talked him through the escape. It was Mia Rain on his implant comms, with XO Anwar running the extraction. Even if his own brain was fried and fogged, surely those two women could tell him what had transpired.

Miles looked over to see Mia Rain and Aisha Anwar at the officers' table, both whispering as they looked at him. Then he felt a sudden hand on his shoulder.

He was surprised to look up and see it was Amestoy. Her hands were surprisingly small, compared to the heft that they had when inside armored gloves. Her ruby nail touched the side of his jaw as she inspected his M5 chip baseplate. "Look at you," she said. "Permanent plate now. Mia's gonna turn you into her own little marionette."

"Yeah, I was wondering that, ma'am," said Miles. "How come none of the rest of the away team have implant baseplates? I can't be the only one at high-risk."

"Oh, I do," said Amestoy. "Mine's not on my neck."

Miles wondered if he would ever see it. "Ma'am," he said, acclimating to her hand's continued presence on his shoulder. "Thanks for having the team get me out of that shithole house. I owe you. And I won't compromise my operational integrity like that again."

"Oh, don't say that," said Amestoy. "You'll do much worse. We all will. That's how people are. But, this time, you made it home alive."

Miles swallowed. Her answer was not at all reassuring. "What was it you wanted to say to me, ma'am?" he asked, turning more to face her. "I assume you came over here for a reason."

Amestoy looked back over at Mia and Aisha, then swallowed. "Yes," she said. "I wanted to know if you'd like to pick the movie we're screening in the briefing room tonight. I thought it would be fair, since you're the big hero today, and you've never picked before."

"Oh," said Miles. "Uh, anything. Whatever you think, really. I'm not a movie guy."

* * *

Miles caught XO Anwar in the hallway after dinner. She was slipping out, and he had to half-run to catch the hijab-wearing woman before she could retreat to her private bunk. "Ma'am," he said, having barely spoken more than a dozen words to her since he started. "XO Anwar, ma'am, I wanted to ask you about my extraction. My memory's shot from the time dilators, but I know you were on the wire for that op. Did anything... happen? I mean, I remember running out the back door. I remember shooting. And..."

"There was dispute between the two gang factions during a drug handoff," said the XO. "It got hot, and you ran out while they were firing at each other."

The obviousness of her lie astounded him. So too did the fact that he could not easily refute her. He *knew* that he had seen black-masked officers in that house, and he had a horrible feeling that he may have killed one in his escape. Still, all those thoughts were dream-like, and he certainly didn't want to press them against XO's word without further proof. "Thank you, ma'am," he said, and let her continue her hasty retreat from the common rooms.

* * *

Captain Amestoy's handset rang on a private line toward the end of the meal. "Excuse me," she said to the officers' table, stepping into the hall before putting the device to her ear. "Amestoy," she said, her go-to greeting for all unknown numbers. "Speak."

The sniveling, unsure voice of a Bertie Lessing came through. "Ah, yes, hello," he said, sounding as if he were gnawing on his hand. "Corrine, was it? From this evening."

"Yes," said Amestoy.

"Right," said Bertie. "Well, you should know we're very grateful for what you did tonight. The republic officers have been telling us all about it."

Captain Amestoy leaned against the bulkhead, sighing to herself as she listened to the man ramble on with flattery. "It's part of the job," she said. "Don't mention it."

"Of course," said Bertie. "And, on that note, that note being jobs, I'd like to put forward an offer. You see, we have no idea how many other nuts like him are out there. We think it would be prudent to bring you on as our head of security. Four-hundred-thousand credits starting, plus expenses. Full time. You would accompany Honey on the road and run the local operations at each venue."

The captain let this hang in silence for a handful of seconds. Then she spoke. "Put her on the line."

Bertie hesitated, perhaps wondering whether or not to pretend Honeyblossom was not there. Then there was a shifting sound, and the voice of Hannah Dunn came through. "Yes?" the singer said, affecting disinterest.

"Head of security?" said Amestoy. "Really, baby?"

She heard Honeyblossom whisper to Bertie, followed by the sound of a closing door. "Well, yes," said the singer. "For all the reasons he said. Of course, we'd need to keep up appearances, but… there would be a lot of extra time, in between."

"I'm not a guard dog," said Amestoy. "And I'm not a shoulder to cry on. Go find someone else to clean you up after you grin and bear it for Duncan Cole."

The captain heard a yelp of sadness and pain on the other side of the line. Then it turned to heavy breathing. Then a bitter snarl. "You spacer mutt," Honeyblossom hissed, saying what she had to say to not be swallowed by despair. "You'll have your fun until some scrapper blows you out of the sky and sells the parts. Then you'll be forgotten just like everyone else in the outworld. You could have been someone. I'm offering you a step up into a world you couldn't dream of. Who the fuck are you, 'Corrine,' to tell me you're too good for it?"

The captain bit back the small urge to tear her apart. "Honey," she said lightly, "I'm just doing what I want. It's a shame you'll never get to know how great that can be."

Then she closed the handset line, ending her connection with Honeyblossom without waiting for a response.

* * *

With Miles declining to choose a film, Amestoy extended the invitation to Lex—who picked the gritty, glitzy, neon-colored action flick *Gangbusters*. "You want some more?" a Juped-out dude in a torn suit shouted, firing an M81 rifle into a bunch of cartel goons on the steps of his coreworld mansion. The rest of the plot continued in similar fashion.

Aurora's 'briefing room' was an onboard private movie theatre, a hangover from the cruiser's days as a luxury yacht. Tonight, as it sometimes did after hard assignments, the room was serving in its original capacity.

Sixteen leather loveseats faced the movie screen in four rows. Ten of *Aurora's* twenty-eight-strong complement had nestled in, so there was plenty of space for the various cliques of the crew to stake their own little claims.

Captain Amestoy sat in the center of the back row, her arm around Grace Burdette's shoulder. In the third row, the cockpit crew munched popcorn and laughed, along with now-plainclothed Lex and Joe. "Hey," said Miles, waiting for Ana Sofia to slide over and make space.

"Hey," she said, but did no such thing.

Leaving her be, Miles wandered forward, until he caught April and Nicki's eyes in the middle of the mostly-empty second row. "Miles!" said April, waving at him as a shuttle explosion roared onscreen. "C'mere. I was just talking about you."

"Oh?" said Miles, and hurried to duck his head at Ropeburn's urging. He sat alone on the first loveseat, separated by two leather arms from April and Nicki in the next one over.

"Hi," said Nicki stiff as she ever seemed to be. She hushed under the dialogue as Orson and Ropeburn quoted each corny line aloud, to their own amusement. "I can't believe you got to meet April's hometown friends before me. She's been talking about them for years."

"Just that guy Mele," said Miles, talking to both of them. "He was cool."

A weird sort of feeling twisted his stomach as he traded cold pleasantries with Nicki. He got the sense that she didn't know about Mia's game, or his rendezvous with April just two hours before. He didn't like the feeling of holding those details back. Instead, he focused on the film, watching wave after wave of bad guy fall in increasingly goofy fashion.

After even two weeks of combat experience, something about the caricature violence on screen now rang false. He thought back to the favorite war movies of his youth, the ones where a young Lord Stahl would run through fire to save a wounded buddy on some distant planetside beach. He wondered if those scenes, too, would seem equally ridiculous if he re-watched them now.

Somewhere within the rice beer and pasta, a lingering concern gnawed at him. It wasn't Nicki, or the film, but the question of the police raid that Aisha Anwar had so plainly dismissed. Forty minutes in, he glanced back to see if Amestoy was still there. She was, and with no Grace Burdette in sight she seemed to be alone.

April's hand had lay on the armrest next to his, a strange half-inch away from touching him, since he'd first sat down. She glanced up as she watched him stand now, smiling politely in the dark. "Bye," said Nicki Stafford, and Miles waved as he cleared out of Ropeburn's line of sight.

Ana Sofia again gave Miles a cold shoulder as he passed her. Reaching the back row, Miles slid in next to the captain. It was only as he was just about seated that he saw Grace's platinum hair in the dim of the theatre. She was on her knees on the floor of the aisle, resting her head on the lap of Amestoy's casual uniform trousers. Both were fully dressed, and Grace seemed almost asleep as Amestoy slowly stroked her ear.

"Oh, excuse me," said Miles, gesturing toward the aisle to ask if he should go.

"Sit," said the captain, and he sat close beside her. It was the nearest to his captain that he'd ever been, and he adjusted to make sure that his own leg was not pressed too tight against hers.

"I've been having some concerns, about the mission," said Miles. His even, measured tone fit nicely with the rising strings of *Gangbusters'* manhunt scene.

Amestoy said nothing, and after thirty seconds he went on. "It's the house I was taken to. I know that wasn't part of our objective. It was my mistake. But, when I was there, Medic Rain hit me with a stim through my M5 chip. I think she was trying to get me out alive, like there was someone trying to kill me and she needed my reflexes sharp. Ma'am, the more I think about it… the more I think I might have killed a cop. Not a newkie, but a real fed. I think they were raiding the house."

"I was off comms," said Amestoy. "XO Anwar handled the extraction. Speak to her."

"I did," said Miles. "She told me it was just a deal gone bad. Respectfully, I find it hard to believe she's telling me the truth. I was thinking of asking Medic Rain about it, but, I thought I should speak to you first."

The captain nodded and considered. "I see," she said, putting both hands on Grace's silver-blonde head as she worked through her thoughts. Then she pressed the pressed lawyer's face down into the warm cotton of her uniform crotch, covering the woman's ears with her inner thighs. "What do you think of Grace?" she asked. "She has an interest in you."

"Ma'am—"

"It's under control, Meyrich," said Amestoy, snapping slightly to close the discussion.

Miles pressed on. "Ma'am, I know you and XO Anwar

might be trying to protect me. Or I might be psyched and hallucinating. But, if I really did that, even in self defense… I would want to know. I wouldn't want kept from me."

"It's under *control*," said the captain, curter now than she'd ever been with him. "This is bigger than you, Operator. Let the game play out."

13 - SMOKE GETS IN YOUR EYES

Miles spent the rest of the movie next to Amestoy and Grace. He wanted her to see him brood, and he didn't really want to join whatever whispered argument April and Nicki had started having in the second row. He crossed his arms, glad to have his own body back after five days under Mia Rain's endocrine control. As a bank tower exploded and the hero saved the day, the concern kept him from drifting into sleep.

Idolex told me. It sent the guns. The ticket. Miles heard the desperate croak of the crazed assassin's voice replay in his head as the credits rolled. Whatever that meant, it was a mystery for those republic men in black to piece together. Still, he couldn't help but think of the remorse the shooter had shown, even in the moment. *Idolex. The guns. It sent the guns. What the hell is 'it?'*

As the lights came up, Miles tapped the black-dressed and moody cyberwarfare operator Caleb Li. Caleb was twenty-six, hung up on music and fashion that had fallen out of date when Miles was a middle schooler. Still, he had a certain moral conviction to his reclusive passions, and Miles knew he could be trusted in a bind. "Caleb," he said, "next time we're on shore leave, remind me. There's something I want your help looking into."

"Sure," said Caleb, who was finishing up telling a joke to Ana Sofia and Orson. "Sure, man. What is it?"

Miles' eyes glanced across the faces of the cockpit crew, who were now all looking him over. "Nothing," Miles lied. "Just some family stuff. I'd rather not get into it on deck."

"For sure," said Caleb, giving Miles a sympathetic pat. "For sure, let me know."

Orson followed Caleb out the door, asking questions about a part of the movie he'd apparently slept through. Miles followed, lagging behind a little, and in the hall just outside the briefing room her heard Nicki Stafford whispering to April in a harsh tone.

"You have no fucking sense of control," hissed Nicki. "You're flailing—"

"I'm living my life—"

"And I'm scared for you!" said Nicki. To Miles shock, she shoved April, fuming in a moment of controlled anger. "Nobody else is gonna take care of you if you shut me out, April. Nobody else is ever gonna stay once they see all that baggage."

April's face had a mix of disappointment, heartbreak, and disgust. "You know what, I used to believe that," said the engineer, "and it fucked with me for a long time, Nicki. I can't believe you let me go on thinking all this bullshit was me, and not your insecurities."

The two of them noticed Miles overhearing, turning away with angry frowns. He should have known better than to gape dumbly at the arguing couple. *Well, if not a couple, then whatever the hell kind of broken mess they are.*

Ana Sofia exited the briefing room, hands in the pocket

of her trademark orange hoodie. She wore sweats and sneakers, and her hair hung long and straight across her chestnut shoulders in brown strands. Miles nodded at his roommate, expecting another rebuff, but she poked him in the gut and gave a sweet half-smile. "Hey *hermano,*" she said, squaring up with him. "I'm going up to my smoke spot. You should come."

Miles checked the time. It was already well past one in the morning, and he hadn't slept since early dawn. "Sure," he said, rallying at her offer. "Sure, I'm game."

* * *

Ten minutes later, Miles climbed a ladder into the work shafts of *Aurora's* upper hull, following Ana Sofia into the five-foot-high, attic-like space. It was crazy for him to think how quickly this ship had gone from a job interview site to a home.

He already felt half-stoned just from exhaustion. Looking up as he climbed, he watched Ana Sofia's full ass shift and bounce in her sweats as she made it to the top of the ladder. As his roommate, she had become ignorably typical—yet somehow still alluring in sheer feisty spirit.

A condenser on one side chilled the air, while a duct on the opposite end of the space kept it warm. In the middle, there was a three-and-a-half-foot Goldilocks Zone, and both privateers squeezed into it on the metal floor.

"You wanna see why this is the best smoke spot on the ship?" asked Ana Sofia.

"Sure," said Miles. "You mean it's not my wonderful company?"

Ana Sofia snorted a laugh and raised her arm up high, causing her hoodie to reveal a thin waist with the tiniest hint of love handles. Then she pulled a panel back, and all at once the vacuum of space was above them.

The thin, sparkling energy of an atmospheric holding field was the only thing separated them from the void beyond. With a touch, Miles could have broken it, sending air streaming out of *Aurora's* hull as they struggled to free his arm and shut the panel. *That* would have been a load of trouble.

"Holy shit," he said, with a moment of panic as he saw the majestic starfield above. It felt almost like seeing the cosmos through a backyard treehouse. "Please close that."

Ana Sofia obliged, and shut the panel before rolling a fresh-smelling blunt. Already, the scent threw him back to hazy, joy-filled second-year days and nights in the Elektra dorms. "Tough shit about the baseplate," she said, licking the edge of the paper to seal the blunt shut. It took him a moment to remember what she was talking about.

"Oh, yeah," he said, touching at the silicon stuck against his neck. "Well, one day I won't be doing field ops any more. I just gotta make sure Mia takes it out before I retire."

"Retire," said Ana Sofia, *"Dios mío."*

She lit the blunt with a small, flame-decaled blue-plasma lighter. If Miles had seen it anywhere onboard, he would have instantly known it was hers. No one, with the exception of Lex, had as brashly tacky taste as Pilot Ana Sofia Serrano–and Lex was a far cry from her hot rod chola persona.

With two puffs, she got it going. Then she passed the smoking blunt to Miles. Already, it was hazing up the small crawlspace, and he knew he was going to end up baked no matter how little he smoked. "If Maeslon tries to drag me out for PT tomorrow," he said, passing it back after two long hits that scorched his throat, "I'm gonna kick her ass. I don't care if she's five-one. I'm a goddamn republic hero. Isaac Stahl said."

"You gotta check yourself," said Ana Sofia. "You

already got big balls, pretty boy. Big balls plus big head equals one dead privateer."

'Pretty boy' made his mind jump back to thirty-year-old Yolanda in the festival toilet. He wondered if she'd survived François, or the black-masked figures that he swore had charged the safehouse. It really didn't seem too likely.

A finger-snap in his face from Ana Sofia roused him, reminding him to pass the blunt again. "You're off in space," she said, facing him as she sat against a bulkhead. He sat opposite, feet outstretched. Their legs overlapped enough that she almost touched his crotch with her red-painted toe. "C'mon, I didn't bring you up here just to watch you play with your own memories."

Miles smiled. His skin felt weird, and it felt even weirder to touch the environment around him. He slid his fingers on the metal, then his own pants, before resting his hand on her foot and rubbing at the sole with his left thumb. It was a warm, reassuring feeling to hold her after so much chaos.

"I fucked a girl in a toilet at the festival," he said. It felt better to say it than to let it keep spinning around in his skull. "Well, a woman. It was a dare from Medic Rain—who is sort of insane, by the way."

"I've heard stories," said Ana Sofia. She seemed to have a genuine, focused interest in his concern and wellbeing. It was a welcome change from the strange, side-eyed flirts and complicated politics of the day. "Were you drunk?"

"No," said Miles. "No, I wouldn't drink on duty."

"But you'd fuck."

"Like Amestoy doesn't?"

Ana Sofia passed the blunt back, and with the new hits Miles could feel his grip on reality starting to melt into a warm puddle. His hand on her soft foot was his only tangible link to the present moment. "Anyway," said the pilot. "Who was she? Festival MILF?"

"No, I wish," said Miles. "She was a fucking gangbanger. Some local biker sort of bullshit. Her guys rammed the toilet with a truck right on the edge of the goddamn festival grounds. Threw me in the back and took off."

"And nobody stopped them?" said Ana Sofia. "No security? Damn, I knew the newkies were a joke, but…"

"I guess," said Miles. His sense of speech, thankfully, was one of the last things to go whenever he smoked or imbibed. "I guess, I dunno."

The pilot adjusted to sit cross-legged, pulling her foot away. Its ghost lingered for a moment as Miles looked down, confused as to where his bit of warm contact had gone. She laughed a little, still half-sober from her own much-higher tolerance. "Well, tough luck," said Ana Sofia. "You screwed around a little. Got thrown in a jam, and the team got you out. If shit had really hit the fan, it would've been Rain that Amestoy nailed to the wall, not you. The doc outranks you, anyway."

"She does?" said Miles, laughing at the thought of it. "Does she outrank you?"

"She's an officer," said Ana Sofia. "Haven't you seen her over at the big girls' table?"

Miles sputtered again, laughing at something that wasn't even that funny. "She, she, she's like a little baby," he said, stopping to thank Ana Sofia as she ashed the blunt in a plastic cup. "She's nineteen. She should be going to, you know, prom or whatever."

"How old are you, eighteen?" said Ana Sofia.

"Yeah," said Miles, contemplative at this. He had forgotten his own self for a moment. "Yeah, maybe I should be at prom, too. Dressing up. Mom and dad taking pictures. You know, this, uh, this gang chick, she was only the second woman I've ever fucked. I mean, properly fucked, like, in the pussy, I mean."

"Yeah, I know fucking," said Ana Sofia. "You've only been with two girls, huh? How many guys?"

"Three girls," said Miles. "No guys."

Ana Sofia blinked, and Miles blinked with her. Now he'd gotten into something he hadn't meant to share. "Three," she said. "So there's someone else you fucked between this afternoon and now? Oh, please don't let it be who I think it is."

"Who do you think it is?" said Miles, doing an extremely bad job at faking coy.

"You know who I think it is," said Ana Sofia, figuring it out with annoyance as she stared at his glassy-eyed face. "Oh, it is who I think it is, too. Oh no, Miles."

"What?" said Miles. "What, don't 'oh no' me. They're not even together. She told me."

"Okay, actually, that could be a lot of people on this ship," said Ana Sofia. "We *are* talking about—"

"April Zamora—"

"April Zamora, yeah," said Ana Sofia. "That fucking *loquita*."

"Hey," said Miles. "Hey I don't know what you're saying, but it's rude, so stop. She's a perfectly fine, kind person."

"Did she tell you she'd never been with a guy before?"

"Yeah," said Miles, rising to meet her snark with indignation. "Yeah, and she, and she said that you tease her about it. You and everyone onboard. Why, was she lying?"

"No, that's true," said Ana Sofia. " At least as far as I know. It's not mean though, you know, what we say to her.

She's just sensitive. We all say that stuff, about everyone. Ropeburn's drunk. Aisha's boring. I'm—"

"A slob?" said Miles.

"I was gonna say a slut," said Ana Sofia.

"I don't think anyone thinks you're a slut," said Miles. "You only ever fuck Orson. I mean, as far as I know. But, come on, that's like an order of magnitude less than most people here."

Ana Sofia softened in an oddball, genuine smile. "You don't think I'm a slut?" she asked, as if he was the first person to ever not lay into her for it.

"No, no, I don't," said Miles. "And that's not the point, I mean, even if I did, like, so what? I mean, I mean, what's wrong with sluts? And, like why would it be anyone's business? That's what I'm saying. And I'm saying to lay off April, too. I mean. She's a psychic, right? Or, reader, whatever they fucking call themselves. So you can't pretend like she's just misunderstanding you."

They had at this point finished the blunt, and Ana Sofia put it out in the plastic ash cup. The air was still thick with haze, perpetually swirling as warm and cold air shifted back and forth. "You are not at all what I expected from a baby blue," said Ana Sofia.

"Well, we're not all the same," said Miles. "I mean, if you'd brought on my partner, Carlotta…"

He trailed off, almost slumping, and Ana Sofia roused him. "Partner who?" she asked, giggling now. She was starting to fall into her own comfortable mush. "What? Who's this girl?"

"No one," said Miles, sighing. "Someone I knew in school."

Ana Sofia re-extended her legs, again pressing hers

against his as her feet came back into reach. "So, now that you tried it a few times. You like it?"

"What?" said Miles. "What, sex?"

"Yeah."

"Yeah," he said, shrugging and laughing. "I mean, everyone does."

"No."

"Oh, well, yeah," said Miles. "I don't know about Engineer Miyachi."

"Can you imagine?" said Ana Sofia, leaning in with gossipy excitement as she put the words together. "Listen, I don't go for girls, but… I don't know. That seven-foot woman, with that cyborg stuff. Sometimes I wonder what she looks like, down there, you know. I've never seen her in the showers."

"I think I'd need to work up to her," laughed Miles. "I feel like her and KALI would be the biggest challenges on the ship. Y'know, 'cause KALI's just a floating steel torso, or a disembodied voice in the hall, or—"

"Hey KALI," said Ana Sofia, speaking to the air. "If you were a real girl would you want to fuck Operator Meyrich? Now that he's got some experience under his belt."

No response came. "Oh yeah," she said. "There's no intercom speakers in here."

"Can she hear us, though?" asked Miles.

"Fuck if I know," said Ana Sofia. "Ask her later I guess."

"What about you?" said Miles, turning her question around. "Do you like it? I would hope so, considering the filth you and Orson leave, uh, leave around the bunk. And, unless he was just shit-testing me that time when he offered, you know…"

"When he said you could fuck my face?"

"Yeah, that," said Miles. "From that I gotta figure you guys are at least a little open."

Ana Sofia shrugged. "Yeah," she said, "I guess. We play like that sometimes. Never solo, though. I'd kick his ass if I caught him with some *puta*."

The thought of squishy, curvy Ana Sofia trying to kick that behemoth's ass made him laugh. He couldn't stop laughing, and he held up a hand to apologize as he half rolled onto the floor in a fit.

"Anyway," said Ana Sofia. "It's been two years together, you know. Stuff gets weird."

"Two years?" said Miles. "That's as long as, what are their names. Nicki and April."

"What a lover you are, can't remember her fuckin' name," Ana Sofia shot back. "Don't compare me to those cat ladies. Aren't you the one who said they're not even together? Maybe you're just trying to cover your own little conscience, homewrecker."

"If April fucks me that's on her," Miles snapped back. "I don't know 'Nicki Stafford.' Whoever the fuck she is. Just the girl that signs my expense reimbursements. If anything it's on Medic Rain for setting up the whole fuckin' mind-game thing."

"The doc made you fuck her?"

"Yeah, it was nuts," said Miles, letting it all spill now. "I come in. She's strapped to this fuckin' operating table thing. Totally naked. She'd agreed to it, I mean, I talked to her there. But I didn't know what the fuck I was walking into. And she didn't know it was gonna be me."

Ana Sofia looked almost excited at his story. She let her mouth fall slightly open, wide eyes and incredulous as he went on. "So how was it?" she asked. "I mean, better than the gangbanger?"

Miles couldn't help but let a victorious, lusty smile fall from his mouth. "Oh you wouldn't believe it," he said. "It was fucking amazing."

Across from him, Ana Sofia's legs tensed. He watched one hand of hers absent-mindedly fall to her crotch, the base of her thumb squishing into the spot just below her pubic mound. Then she took a big, half-sobering breath and handed him the plastic ash cup. "I'll meet you down there," she said, releasing the hatch down to the rest of the ship. "Your girl needs a little time to tend to herself."

14 - INTERPOLITICS

Captain Amestoy found Nicki Stafford sobbing alone at a mess hall table at three in the morning. The captain had gone for a late-night run, not yet able to clear her mind of the quagmire that surrounded the latest mission. After four miles pounding the ship gym's treadmill, some balance had returned, and she was able to look on the frizzy-haired accountant with some sympathy as she chugged a pre-made peanut butter protein shake.

"Hi Captain," said Nicki, sniffing as she tried to compose herself. She wore a grey hoodie over a video game themed tee, the same sort of perpetually sophomoric look that she'd sported since coming onboard *Aurora* two years prior. For all the drama and heartbreak and growth that had wracked the rest of the team, twenty-six-year-old Nicki Stafford seemed to be in a state of perpetual developmental paralysis.

"Hi Nicki," said Amestoy. "Rough night, huh?"

Nicki nodded. Her hair was bushy even when pulled back, and it bounced in a light brown ponytail as she wiped her nose.

"Yeah," said the captain. "I've been thinking about what you said, about Honeyblossom. About what she did to you back at CYU."

"Yeah," said Nicki. "It sucked. But I'm sure she's grown up now. Did you meet her?"

"I did," said Amestoy. "She's still the same brat."

"She kinda ruined my life, for a little bit," said Nicki. "I'm even starting to wonder if we dated. I mean, I know we did. I know what we did. But she said so many horrible lies, about me, about hating the thought of touching a woman."

The captain nodded. "Would it make you feel better," she asked carefully, "to see her admit it in a… compromised position?"

A slight smile blossomed on Nicki's exhausted face. "Oh, it would," she said.

"Come with me," said Amestoy, leading Nicki first to the armory then the bridge. She'd picked up her combat helmet, which Orson had collected for her after she'd left it in Honeyblossom's concert hall dressing room. Then, at Caleb's cyberwarfare terminal, the captain plugged the helmet in and decrypted its stored audiovisual logs.

A helmet-cam feed started up, tracing hours of bureaucracy as the taxi landed on the New Canberran pad. From her own perspective, Amestoy re-watched herself punching the extortionist newkie. Then Ji-Yoon showed up, and after another bit of scrubbing she watched the helmet be set down on Honeyblossom's hotel suite bookshelf.

The position of the helmet now overlooked the bed. She scrubbed ahead a bit further, hearing Nicki gasp and lean in closer as Honeyblossom's half-dressed form appeared onscreen. The boys appeared, then Alex ate her out, then Amestoy spoke with Toshi and all of a sudden

Honeyblossom was chasing the two boys out of the room.

"They look just like two kids she and I had in our cohort," Nicki laughed, astonished. "One's an investment banker now. The other does venture capital. Both of them fucking hated Hannah. Man, she's really insane. I wonder who else she's searched up a lookalike for."

"Here we are," said Amestoy, setting an in-point to the video. She jumped ahead an hour, set an out-point, and exported the subsequent clip to a portable card. "Watch it on your own time," she told Nicki, putting in the card in her hands. "And don't let it spread around. That's *Aurora* classified property."

"It lives and dies with me," said Nicki, flipping the card over and over in her hands. She now looked like a kid who couldn't want to open a birthday gift. "Wow, what a weird night. Thank you, ma'am. This means a lot."

"Dismissed," said the captain, and remembered that she'd left Grace Burdette in the master quarters for an hour.

* * *

Miles had idled at the bottom of the ladder for a few minutes after climbing down. He stood at the end of a dark hallway, off a service corridor which connected to the third-floor stairwell. The chaff pod and shield generator access points, and Captain Amestoy's suite, were the only things of real note on this level.

His handset chimed with a message on a public channel. He fumbled for it, at first holding the screen upside down. Then he focused his eyes on the glare to see the name 'Carlotta Toro.'

He guffawed, and his outburst prompted Ana Sofia's voice from the half-open smoke spot hatch above. "Who is it?" she asked, in what was either a murmur of stoned confusion or pleasure.

"That partner I mentioned," said Miles. "The one from school."

He opened the message, and his surprise turned into disbelief. It read: 'stuck in my combat suit legs again. big design flaw. wish someone could help me out here, or smthn…'

His memories of their last encounter—his first time ever—washed over him. "Don't respond while you're, while, while you're faded," said Ana Sofia, mumbling from above as she heard him laugh.

"I won't," said Miles, and shut his handset again. "Goodnight, roomie."

He took ten wobbly steps forward, and was about to continue downstairs when he saw a shrouded figure in the dark on the other side of the corridor. A loud power cell separated them, and she couldn't hear him approaching as he crept around the wall to get a better look.

As he neared, he could see that a panel separating the hall from the master suite had been pulled back, and that the shrouded figure silently peeking through it was XO Aisha Anwar.

* * *

Aisha knew she had no business being up here. She knew there were more reasonable hours to check the interface panels, and she knew that there was no reason for a panel check to require the whole wall unit be pulled aside. Still, here she was, watching the bed of the master suite through a small electrical gap.

Inside the room, Grace Burdette sat back on the bed, bottomless in her shirt and blazer. She stared at the holo-wall, pushing a buzzing, ball-shaped massager into her naked crotch.

"When I was twenty," a woman on the holo-wall said,

just out of view from Aisha's hallway vantage point, "my parents sent me to a convent. I was losing my mind. I wanted to fuck the statues. The crosses. Anything. Three weeks in, another sister was caught with some Jupiter from town. She was already on her last strike before expulsion. That was going to be it. So I went to her one night as we were cleaning the crypts, in this sort of sex-blinded state, and I told her I would say the Jupe was mine if she licked my pussy."

"Oh…" Grace moaned, rocking back and adding another hand to the motion.

"I don't even know if she knew she was gay," the woman on the holo-call went on. "But she knelt down right there and ate my bush out on the steps of the crypts. We fucked all over that place for the next three years, until I left to go into colonial development. I'm pretty sure she's still there, too. Who knows who she's fucking now."

Aisha felt a locked, overwhelming tunnel-vision overtake her as she watched Grace Burdette pleasure herself on the bed. The XO knew that any exploration of her own lust was forbidden. It was a virtue she valued, and one she intended to maintain until the beautiful day that her future marriage vows were consummated. Still, she was equally called by her faith to embrace scientific inquiry, and there was some value in understanding just what it was that made Burdette act this way…

She slipped her lightly cotton-gloved hand under the fabric of her patterned shawl and casual uniform pants. Comparing herself to the murky shape of Grace, she made a little space in her underwear and lightly touched the spot where she thought the center of the massager's pressure might be.

The rush of pleasure that came was not alien to her, nor was it entirely surprising. Still, the suddenness of the thrill, combined with the vicious urge to press more and more against herself until she could not stand, was alarming in its new intensity.

Across the room from Grace, the master suite's door opened, and Captain Amestoy entered in her workout wear. Aisha had picked her hiding place well, and she knew there was no way for Amestoy to see her easily from the threshold or the bed.

"Who's this?" said the captain, asking Grace about the woman on the holo-screen.

"That's, uhm," Grace moaned. "That's…"

"I'm Miriam," said the unseen woman. "And that's my wife, Carli, in the cage."

The captain stuck her fingers in Grace's mouth, pushing her back as she straddled her. "You got a little head start, huh?" she asked, then moved her fingers to take off her own exercise top.

Aisha almost couldn't contain her excitement. This was, though she would never admit it to herself, the moment she had been waiting for since she had made plans to open the panel earlier that night. The thought of Captain Amestoy naked, displaying her muscles and her power without hesitation as she had her way with a woman, was something that lingered the very core of XO Aisha Anwar's consciousness at all times.

Then, just before Amestoy could remove her top, another call came through the master suite's line. "Fuck!" the captain shouted. "Fuck. Fuck me. Miriam, another time." With a slam on the bedstand console, she shut off the holo-screen. "Grace, out."

* * *

Miles, in his stoned stupor, had been standing in the hall watching XO Anwar for he-didn't-know-how-long. He was amazed that she hadn't seen him there, and more amazed that she seemed to be touching herself beneath her pants and shawl. "I guess I'll keep you off the list with Evelyn and KALI," he mumbled barely-audibly to himself. "Just goes to show everyone's got surprises."

Then the side-door of the master suite opened, and suddenly Grace Burdette was slipping right past him down the hall. He glanced to Aisha—who had jumped into the shadows with fright at the sound of the door. Somehow, Grace noticed neither of them in the dark, and Miles heard a vibrator buzz against Grace's clit as she walked down the stairs to the second-floor hall.

Then Miles approached the XO. "Operator," she whispered, bolting the panel shut in embarrassment. "This is an officers' wing. Go to sleep."

"I was just, I was, up," Miles mumbled, giggling as he pointed to the hatch behind him. He couldn't explain his evening in a way that would make any sense. "I just need to get my balance, and I'll go."

The XO nodded, breathless and flustered, doing her best to keep on a face of stern propriety. "Carry on," she said. "I need to find a soldering gun to repair this panel."

Anwar hurried down the stairs toward the armory, out of sight. Alone, Miles stumbled softly forward, picking at the latch which she'd frantically slipped shut. As he had suspected, it opened to reveal a discreet view into the captain's cabin.

Peering through the gap, he saw Corrine Amestoy angrily pacing as she snapped at someone new on the holo-screen. "Isaac, it's a fucking disgrace. You set us up. We could have been killed."

"But you came out alive," said Lord Stahl's voice. It had none of the pomp and bravado here that it had on New Canberra, or in his old films. "And in fact it was one of *my* guys, one of my best guys, that got killed by your incompetent fucking operator."

"Your guy was dirty as sin," said Amestoy, "just like this whole deal. And my operator did what anyone would do in that situation. Any cop, any bounty hunter, any merc, any civilian. Someone kicks in a door and tries to kill you, you kill back. How could I know that hole he fell into was the same one your mooks were planning to toss? You know how many shitholes like that there are in New Canberra?"

"You could have brought in a team that understands the sensitivities—"

"My crew are good people," said Amestoy. "That's part of why they get results. If they don't believe in the mission, Isaac, they're out. So up until now I've said what I needed to say to get things done. But that's over. I'm through with your dirty work."

"It's a shame to hear that," said Lord Stahl. "We did some impressive work together… even if you do run a ship of fools."

It wasn't clear in his tone if Lord Stahl's words came as a threat. "You try to take us out of the game," the captain warned him, jabbing a finger at the screen as her bare abs flexed, "and you'll be staring at five hundred dead feds minimum before you've seen the last of us."

"Quite a threat for a woman who's just decided she's on the righteous path," Stahl laughed. "Luckily for both of us, Corrine, you're small time. We have no need to take *Aurora* out of anything. You'll simply fade away, another one of the thousands of bounty ships trawling the outworld for a couple of credits."

Miles heard new steps coming up the aft stairs. He shut the panel again, slipping away, and tried to cross the corridor toward the stairs in the fore. Instead, he ran into bottomless Grace Burdette in the dark of the hall.

He heard the vibrator-ball buzzing in her hand, pressed up against her as she stared at him. "You're not supposed to be up here," she smiled, a foot away from him.

"No," said Miles, too brain-fucked by the weed and what he'd heard to say anything else.

She let a moment linger, trying to read his face. There was way too much going on in his head for her to possibly put a finger on it. "I should get back to Captain," she said at last. "If she's done."

"Yeah?" said Miles, remembering the mess she'd made of herself at his onboarding. "You're not trying to get together, swap some stories with me anymore?"

"Operator Meyrich, I find you delightful," said Grace, still touching herself as she rested her ass against the cold metal wall. "But you look like death right now, and you reek of pot. Why don't you go downstairs, and I'll see you tomorrow."

Miles nodded, swallowing. If there was anyone with whom he was going to broach the subject of Amestoy's overheard call with Lord Isaac Stahl, it certainly wouldn't be her. For now, he decided, the weight of the situation was so complex and looming that he couldn't even start to process it. It was something for a sober mind to take on, and for his current stoned state to ignore as if he'd never found XO Anwar's hiding spot in the first place.

* * *

The galley was closed, but Miles' clearance allowed him to open the door with his biometric scan. Entering the room, which he'd never been in before, he fumbled around through bins and trays to find the ingredients for a sandwich. "Cop killer," he murmured, and shivered as he spoke the words. "Dirty cops," he said, and that phrase sat more ponderously in the air. "Ravioli," he said, now reading a container, and scarfed down a box of cold pasta before dropping it to the floor.

"KALI," he said, stumbling back out to the empty mess hall, "tell Cook Hansen I'm sorry about his ravioli, when he comes in tomorrow."

"I will pass that along, Operator," said KALI.

Her voice brought an old, renewed question from earlier in the night to his mind. "KALI," he said, are you running surveillance on the whole third floor and crawlspaces?

If asked of a human, this would be a transparently incriminating question. He hoped that the ship's navigation intelligence would not consider it a suspicious line of investigation. "I am only active in the primary second floor hallways and rooms, shuttle bay, power bay, armory, first floor bunks, and master suite," said KALI. "I do not have the capacity to interact with anyone beyond these regions, unless the emergency thermal scanners are turned on in battle mode. I apologize if this is an inconvenience, Operator—"

"No, it's fine," said Miles. "It's fine, thanks, KALI. You have a really pretty voice, you know that? Is it a real person's voice? I mean, 'real.' You know. Human—"

"My voice was designed by Devon Labs, on Tatapani," said KALI. "It is based in part on the voice of actress Tamisha Colfield."

"Oh," said Miles. "I guess that makes sense."

He stumbled to the second-floor barracks showers, which were empty. There, he brushed his teeth, and as he did so he thought back on his various encounters with Carlotta, Yolanda, and April. Then he thought of Ana Sofia touching herself in the crawlspace, and he wondered if there was any part of her that was thinking of him.

At this image, he felt himself get hard beneath his casual uniform trousers. He pressed his own dick, feeling the ridge at the edge of the head through his pants. As good as it felt, he could barely brush his teeth, and knew he had none of the coordination needed to jerk himself off.

He returned to his room and was surprised to find it empty. "Of course," he said, to the imprint of Ana Sofia's ass on her lower bunk mattress. "You're still upstairs."

Miles considered climbing the ladder to his bunk. Then his thoughts returned again to his handset. Grabbing the top of his pants with one hand, he pulled them down until the top of his trimmed pubes were showing. He gripped a fistful and a half of solid dick through the grey fabric.

Barely balancing, he snapped a photo on his handset. Then he opened the conversation open with Carlotta. With a giggle, and against Ana Sofia's clear instructions, he attached the photo he'd just took and sent it through the interspace relays to the eighteen-year-old special forces lieutenant's personal handset.

Somewhere onboard a shitty naval frigate, he imagined her getting the image in her bunk. Maybe an intelligence officer would have to screen it, before it could be sent through. Maybe it would never arrive at all. "I've got a tool that can help with that," he typed out, speaking each word as he wrote with excruciating slowness.

He added a wink for good measure, then set his handset down and lost it in the dark of the room. In pitch black, stripped naked in the cold, he felt almost as if he could be standing in the void of space. "Eerie," he mumbled, and sincerely hoped that his death would not be an airlocking.

The uneven beat of the air vent above clicked like a broken metronome. Climbing the bunk, Miles nestled in, and shut his eyes to a sleep full of fitful, sensual, strange and concerning dreams.

ABOUT THE AUTHOR

Vanessa Park is a television writer and novelist from Los Angeles, California. Before working in fiction, she spent three years on the crew of an ocean research vessel in the South China Sea. She loves genre storytelling, and fills her worlds with the same kind of boundary-pushing adventure she seeks in life.

If you run into her by day, she'll buy you a coffee at one of her Los Feliz hotspots. If you run into her by night, she'll show you the wildest of what her city has to offer.

www.ingramcontent.com/pod-product-compliance
Lightning Source LLC
Chambersburg PA
CBHW060547160726
47991CB00001B/466